FOWLER'S
SNARE

FOWLER'S SNARE

NORMAN MOSS

WORD BOOKS

NELSON WORD LTD
Milton Keynes, England
WORD AUSTRALIA
Kilsyth, Victoria, Australia
WORD COMMUNICATIONS LTD
Vancouver, B.C., Canada
STRUIK CHRISTIAN BOOKS (PTY) LTD
Cape Town, South Africa
CHRISTIAN MARKETING NEW ZEALAND LTD
Havelock North, New Zealand
JENSCO LTD
Hong Kong
JOINT DISTRIBUTORS SINGAPORE -
ALBY COMMERCIAL ENTERPRISES PTE LTD
and
CAMPUS CRUSADE, ASIA LTD
SALVATION BOOK CENTRE
Malaysia

FOWLERS SNARE

© Frontier Publishing International Ltd. 1993

ISBN 0-85009-764-9 (Australia ISBN 1-86258-291-2)

Created, designed and typeset by Frontier Publishing International Ltd., BN43 6RE, England. Reproduced, printed and bound in Great Britain for Nelson Word Ltd. by Cox and Wyman Ltd., Reading.

93 94 95 96 / 10 9 8 7 6 5 4 3 2 1

To our grandchildren

CONTENTS

THE STRANGELANDS

1. Black Tor
2. Drocken Wood
3. Cragrock
4. Chuckle's Cottage
5. Dunroamin'
6. Heartsease
7. Grimvald
8. Diamede
9. Castle

------- Driftwood's Voyages

FARSTRAND

NEARSTRAND

Creek

Potlot

3 days' journey

CHAPTER 1
BLACK TOR

❀

*T*he door of the Tavern crashed back on its hinges with a bang that shook the door posts. A rush of wind from the sea set the oil lamps swinging from the dark beams of the ceiling. A gasp of fear shuddered among the company at the bar. The sea shanty that had been on their lips a moment before ceased abruptly.

All eyes were fixed on the black cloaked figure in the doorway. He stood, his face hidden in the shadows. Then he moved forward. His bodyguards crowded behind him — strong ruthless men with cruel faces. They wore no distinguishing uniform, and in the lamplight only their lacklustre eyes gave any clue to their identity.

'Dreirds,' somebody whispered, and others whimpered with terror.

'On your knees all of you.'

The man's voice had a cold authority. He spoke as one absolutely certain that he would be obeyed. They shrunk away from him in fear. There was a moment of silence so complete that the waves could be heard swishing against the pebbles in the distance — the tide was at the full that night. Glummit's old Grandfather clock ticked once, its heavy brass pendulum swinging steadily. Before it could tick again the jerseyed fishermen, and farm labourers who had been drinking at the bar were falling to their knees in submission to this terrible stranger. From the folds of his robe he produced a flask and a silver chalice. With care he poured the liquid into the cup. Then, holding the chalice aloft he declared,

'The pledge of loyalty — long live King Threld, and Fowler his Viceroy!' Then he ordered 'Get to work Slobbit.'

Slobbit scrambled forward from the doorway — a stooping, hairy, ungainly figure with long arms and hunched and lopsided shoulders. He looked like a man, but was barrel chested almost like a bear. In the lamplight his expression conveyed a mixture of stupidity and slyness. His lips were full and wet, his nose almost broad enough to be a snout. His eyebrows were thick and bushy, and the eyes were strangely disproportioned, one being larger than the other. His hands were gross and paw-like, each with six fingers. The dirty nails had been bitten short.

Slobbit put one finger in the corner of his mouth, pulling the moist lip down, and making a squelching sound. Then he removed the finger with a plop, and moved forward in front of his master. Taking the chalice he motioned to the man kneeling nearest to him.

'You. Drink now.' he grunted. As the man obeyed, Slobbit moved on to the next kneeling figure.

'Congratulations.' sneered Fowler. 'You've pledged loyalty at last. You peasants of Cragrock have been a law to yourselves for far too long. But at last I, Fowler, have you in my power. Obey me, and you and your families will prosper. Offend me, and you will perish. Is that understood?'

Slobbit motioned to the next villager to take the chalice. In a split second Driftwood decided what he would do. Fowler's visit had been rumoured by traders returning from Heartsease. Those who drank the pledge of loyalty became Dreirds, meekly submissive to Fowler's will. Driftwood saw no reason why he should be press-ganged in this way.

With one leap he vaulted over the counter and plunged his hands into the drawer of Glummit's till. Snatching gold, silver, and copper coins, he flung handfuls of them into the middle of the floor. Then without waiting to see the result, he dived through the open window at the end of the bar, and escaped into the night.

Behind him there was pandemonium. Much as the patrons of the Tipsy Goose feared the Dreirds, they were still greedy for money. Most of them were poor, and the sight of scattered gold pieces rolling on the stained floorboards broke the trance of Fowler's presence. With oaths and curses they scrambled over one another, snatching up the coins, stamping on each other's fingers, determined to get their share. Driftwood clambered over a dry stone wall, and made off across the fields. He stayed in the deeper shadows of the hedgerows, following the hidden paths that had been familiar territory to him since early childhood.

Driftwood had no time to feel triumphant about his escape. The situation was still desperate. Glancing over his shoulder as he ran he could see the faintly phosphorescent breath of the Dreirds as they hurried after him. Torches were being lit, and Fowler was snarling orders. There were at least twenty Dreirds, and Slobbit, on hands and knees, was snuffling at the ground to pick up Driftwood's scent. Driftwood vaulted over the five bar gate into the lane, ran between high stone walls, dodged under the arch of a small bridge and splashed his way upstream.

Then he took to the open hillside. He ran as fast as he could, stumbling on hands and knees over boulders, wading through tall bracken that lashed at his face and falling once or twice in the heather. Higher he climbed, until at last he paused by the gaunt standing stones, known as Moses' Tables — grim shapes that had frowned over the landscape from time immemorial. They marked the brooding summit of Black Tor which, according to legend, had power to cast strange terrors.

But Driftwood had never found the place unfriendly. By the time he got there, his chest was heaving with the effort of climbing and the air seemed to be burning his throat as he drew it in with anguished gasps. Sweat was streaming down his forehead and face.

He glanced back towards the Tipsy Goose. In the half light of the moon which was shining among heavy clouds, he could see the wide sweep of the bay, and further still, the darkness of the deep ocean. A few riding lights were burning among the vessels in the harbour and a lightbuoy was flashing silently on the horizon. Below him he heard the distant shouts of the Dreirds — they were calling to one another. He was not sure whether they knew where he was or not, but he took to his heels and fled down into the dark ravine that lay below the crest of the hill. On he ran, till at last he could see home.

To others it might have seemed an eery place; to Driftwood, it was the only home he had ever known. A pillar, built of slabs of grey slate and supported a weathered signboard which read:

Black Tor Quarries
Strug and Stumble
Monumental Masons
Undertakers

Along the stone paved alleyway, a light burned in a ramshackle stone shed. Driftwood ran into the yard shouting for help. Then he rushed into the shed. Strug, humpbacked and squinting, stood with a hammer in one hand and a chisel in the other. He had been cutting lettering into a slate headstone which was leaning against a wall of the shed. Robed statues — some half finished — stood here and there. They brooded in the fitful light, casting strange shadows as the lamp swayed from its iron chain in the rafters. Blocks of slate were littered everywhere.

For all his unsightly appearance, Strug was a master craftsman. In better times he might have been praised as a sculptor, but times were hard and his best trade now came from making funeral monuments.

Driftwood was panting so hard he could hardly speak.

'It's that man, Fowler. He's after me. I've been drinking down at the Tipsy Goose. I know I shouldn't and I'm sorry. But do please hide me! I'm in terrible trouble!'

'Quick, Stumble' cried Strug. 'Help me with the lid of this coffin.'

The two of them heaved at the great lid of a sarcophagus that stood across the shed on a block of fine marble. The lid shifted with a grating sound.

'Get in and look sharp about it. There'll be enough air for someone of your size.'

Driftwood lay in the coffin and gazed up at their anxious, grave and yet kindly faces. They were his guardians, the only parents he could remember. The next moment the lid was over him, and he was entombed in total darkness. It was cold, black, uncomfortable. He knew that the coffin would soon be airless and running with condensation. But at least it was a hiding place. From inside, he could hear his guardians' muffled voices.

'I'll get my blunderbuss' said Stumble — a tall, lean and sinewy man who spent most of his time labouring in the mine. Strug did the more skilled work, although Stumble was actually as expert as his brother.

Stumble took down his weapon from the wooden pegs hammered into the crevices of the shed wall. Strug coolly returned to his chip chip chipping at the lettering on the headstone. They did not have to wait long before two Dreirds appeared in the doorway. One moved to each side of the entrance and stood guard. Their lacklustre eyes stared directly ahead of them and luminous vapour curled from their nostrils. They drew even breaths — in spite of the climb to the quarry. And now, with features impassive, they stood as still and silent as the blocks of sculptured stone.

Strug paused, his hammer raised as if he had suddenly been surprised while at work. Then he thoughtfully weighed his hammer in his hand.

'State your business.' said Stumble from behind the trumpet barrel of his blunderbuss.

The Dreirds neither moved, nor spoke. Strug resumed his work.

'No manners!' he muttered and shook his head with a sigh.

Slobbit lurched through the open door, one finger in his dribbling mouth. He leered at the stonemasons. Behind him, hidden in the shadows, was Fowler.

'Put down your weapon, old man' he said. 'I come with authority from King Threld.'

'State your business then.' grunted Strug. ''Tis late to be calling. We're respectable craftsmen my brother and I. We've worked this quarry for more years than I can remember. Nobody's ever found us disloyal to King Threld.'

'Nevertheless,' said Fowler 'there are two matters. Both will test your boasted loyalty. The second shall be first. It concerns a troublesome boy who escaped from Glummit's Inn tonight. It is said that he lives here at the quarry. He's — inconvenienced me. I'm displeased with him.'

'The first matter concerns your duty. I have decided that you shall have the honour of drinking the pledge of loyalty. Not all are chosen. We were disappointed at the Inn. Glummit and his cronies are pitiful wrecks of men. However we found a few strong mariners, and two sturdy ploughmen. They've joined us. You two have courage. I admire that. And your muscles have become strong with constant toil. I've decided to enlist you.'

'Not so!' said Stumble grimly, as he tightened his grip on his weapon. 'We're far too busy here.'

'Once you've drunk the pledge I shall not trouble you.' Fowler replied calmly. 'You may continue here as before. Your work will be unchanged, your profit will be greater. I'll send you customers. Then one day I'll summon you to Diamede and you'll see King Threld.'

Strug shifted uneasily. He distrusted this stranger. He knew the rumours that circulated about the Dreirds. He didn't believe the promise he was being given, but as a law abiding man he recognised the authority of King Threld.

'Show us your authority.' he demanded.

Fowler passed a small object to a Dreird who stepped forward with impassive face and held out his hand. There was no mistaking the fabulous signet ring that gleamed in his palm. Even in the dim light of the shed it shone and sparkled with inner light. All who saw it recognised it as belonging to Threld. It certified Fowler's right to be obeyed.

Slowly Stumble lowered his blunderbuss. The Dreird returned the ring, and took up his position again. Reluctantly but obediently the two brothers knelt before Slobbit and in turn drank from the chalice.

'Now to the second matter which was first.' continued Fowler. 'The boy — the runaway. That draught you have received brings your will into subjection to mine. You're powerless to resist me. You will speak and tell me the truth.'

Slowly Strug and Stumble rose to their feet. Strug spoke. His face ashen, a slight fleck of foam in the corner of his mouth. Beads of perspiration showed on his forehead, though the shed was cold. But his eyes were fierce. He glared at Slobbit and then shifted his gaze towards the hooded face of his oppressor.

'Listen to me, man of evil.' His voice came with difficulty as if he were speaking through pain. He sounded like a judge pronouncing sentence.

'Long ago, far beyond memory, my brother and I were appointed to labour in Black Tor. Who sent us, or why we're here we cannot recall. For Black Tor itself has become our master.' He continued as though reciting an ancient legend.

'There are two powers, just as there are two mountains. The power of Black Tor, and the power of Diamede. Neither threatens the other for both have been and both shall be. We are men. We honour the authority of King Threld of Diamede. But we're also servants of Black Tor.'

Fowler interrupted.

'What is all this nonsense? Tell me where the boy is. Tell me at once. You cannot resist my power.'

Strug shook his head as one dazed.

'I reserve the right to silence.' he responded. 'I am obedient to King Threld, but not to you. I will answer the King before his throne in Diamede. I will not answer you. Know this and understand it well. Black Tor does not serve us. We serve Black Tor. Sometimes Black Tor awakes, and when it awakes, there is terror. My brother and I do not command this terror.'

He paused and looked at his brother. Their eyes met and a glance passed between them. Very gently Stumble murmured. 'My brother and I sense that Black Tor is awakening now.'

Even as he spoke the ground beneath them trembled as an earthquake shuddered in the depths of the mountain. Then there was a terrible stillness, far more awesome than any noise — a total silence. Even Fowler felt the terror, the sense of dread, of loneliness, of desolate emptiness. The silence clutched at his mind with chill fingers which threatened to tear away all reason.

Suddenly Slobbit whimpered and clutched at his master's feet.

'Slobbit frightened, Master. We go from here.'

He began to sob and groan. Fowler kicked at him angrily. Then the Dreirds at the door were overcome with spasms of shuddering. Their teeth began chattering, and their hands started shaking uncontrollably. With a shriek of terror, one of them turned and ran off into the night. The other followed him, in the process stumbling headlong over Slobbit who was frantically trying to make good his own escape. Outside the Dreirds panic-stricken screams and shrieks faded into the distance as they fled from the silent terror of Black Tor.

Fowler had drawn his cloak about him as if to protect himself.

'So,' he said. 'The legend is right. There is power hidden in Black Tor. All power interests me. I must learn to use this terror. Eventually I will turn it to my own ends. But for tonight I shall withdraw. You men have appealed to King Threld. I will confront you there before his throne. We shall meet again.' Then he was gone.

CHAPTER 2
THE PEARL

"'T is passing strange, brother.' said Strug. "'Twas ever so. Others feel the terror of Black Tor. Yet you and I, and young Driftwood have lived here unharmed.'

'Aye,' Stumble replied. 'Many a villager has run screaming from these slopes. Yet I have laboured in the Tor for as long as I can remember and the terror never touches me. If only ...'

He sighed and passed a hand wearily across his forehead. 'If only I could remember how we came here to begin with.'

'Let be brother,' said Stumble. 'We must release Driftwood. It's safe for the present — while the Dreirds are gripped by the terror. It will probably take Fowler the rest of the night to round them up.'

Together they heaved at the coffin lid. Neither complained, but the potion they had drunk was causing them great weakness and pain. Eventually the lid grated, moved and revealed a wide eyed and still shaken Driftwood. He lost no time in clambering out.

'Have they really gone?' he asked anxiously. He feared that Fowler was playing a trick, and might return at any moment. Stumble reassured him.

'Nay lad, you're safe for now. I've seen the power of the Black Tor at work before. Those gripped by its terrors won't return — no matter what threats Fowler makes. The terror of the Black Tor is the greatest terror. If only I could remember ...' He broke off. Driftwood was staring at the ashen faced Strug.

'You both look so ill.' he cried 'What's happened to you?'

'They call it the pledge of loyalty.' groaned Strug. 'We both had to drink it because we're both loyal to King Threld. Fowler had his signet ring. We couldn't disobey.'

Driftwood shrank back.

'Does that mean you have become Dreirds?' he faltered.

'No.' said Stumble. 'But there's an agony within us. Every moment we have to resist Fowler's will. Even now he's calling us to hand you over to him. But have no fear lad.'Tis old Black Tor. Others fear it, but it strengthens us.'

'Get supper ready, Driftwood.' said Strug. ''Tis late, and there's much to say before sleep comes.'

The three sat down to steaming mugs of soup, a hunk of bread and a lump of cheese. An old lantern stood in the centre of the bench. Driftwood watched the harrowed faces of his guardians whose features were made grotesque by the shadows and by their suffering. They seemed to have aged. He wondered whether the potion would kill them if it couldn't break their wills.

'Fetch the package Stumble!' said Strug.

Stumble lifted a chisel from the bench and went wearily to a corner of the shed. He levered at a stone which moved revealing a small cavity. Carefully he pushed his hand inside and removed a parcel wrapped in oilskin. He paused, and then as if reading his brother's thoughts, stooped again and took out a larger and heavier bag of rough canvas. As he put the bag on the bench beside Strug. Driftwood heard the rattle of many coins.

Strug took a knife from his pocket and pressed the catch, with a click the knife blade sprang into position. Driftwood had always admired that pocket-knife. Strug cut the twine around the smaller package and unwrapped the oilskin to reveal a soft leather pouch. Gently he shook this over the table and out fell a very small pearl. Then with two fingers he fished inside the pouch and brought out a scrap of yellowed parchment.

'We've told you this before Driftwood my lad — how one night after a great storm Stumble and I found you among the boulders of the bay. You were lashed to a beam of timber from a shipwreck — no more than a baby, and nearly dead at that. Soaked to the skin you were, and blue with cold. And this pouch was tied to you.'

'It's a tiny pearl.' said Driftwood. 'It could easily get lost. We wouldn't get much for it if we tried to sell it.'

'Aye lad, you're right' continued Strug. 'Yet some-one thought it important enough to attach to you. Then there's the scrap of parchment.'

Driftwood held the parchment up to the light. He could still read the words faintly inscribed on it: 'HOLD FAST TILL.'

'Till what?' he wondered aloud.

'A meaning there must be.' said Stumble. 'What-ever way you look at it, that pearl is your property — your only property. If I were you I would guard it safely just in case. Who knows? One day the mystery may be solved.'

'You wouldn't try to sell it then?' asked Driftwood.

'Never.' said Stumble. 'My guess is that your poor mother must have tied that to you as she was drown-ing. The parchment tells you to hold it fast, and that's exactly what you must do.'

Driftwood nodded. It didn't seem too important really. After all it was a very small pearl. But he felt a twinge of sadness at the idea of his mother and father being drowned. He would certainly hold on to the pearl. Strug put it and the parchment back into the pouch.

'Hang it round your neck.' he advised. 'We've kept it hidden till now. But tonight has brought great changes, lad. Stumble and I are leaving you tomor-row!'

Driftwood stared at him. 'What do you mean?'

"Tis like this lad. My brother and I must appeal to King Threld. He was always a just ruler — at least until this Fowler creature came on the scene. In the old days the land was quiet and peaceable. Now folks are oppressed. Dreirds burn down cottages. Some people have been taken away, and no one knows what's happened to them. Fowler has more and more power, and now he has even dared to come to Black Tor. He meant to make us his agents here, to turn us into Dreirds who would work for him — maybe as prisoners in the mines. Who knows?'

'Aye there's only one thing we can do' said Stumble 'We must appeal to King Threld himself. He must be able to do something to take the power from Fowler and to undo the power of the pledge of loyalty.'

'But will Fowler let you reach the King?' asked Driftwood. 'Fowler isn't supreme.' grunted Strug. 'King Threld is still the ruler, and we are appealing to him. Fowler can hardly refuse. He doesn't control the whole country — only the Dreirds in his private army.'

'We'll set out tomorrow.' said Stumble, 'and we'll take a present for the King. I know the very thing, Strug. That carving of the two horses. You made it two winters ago. It's one of your best pieces. If we come to the Castle of Diamede bearing a gift for the King, only a bold man would refuse us admission. Once there we must see what the King will say for we are his loyal subjects.'

'I've always wanted to see the castle of Diamede!' Exclaimed Driftwood excitedly.

Strug shook his head.

'You won't be coming lad. Don't you see? You'd be in danger. Fowler wants to get hold of you and turn you

into a Dreird, but he doesn't actually know what you look like. You can be sure that we'll be watched on our journey. If we take a boy with us, he'll know who you are. And once he forced the pledge of loyalty down your throat you wouldn't stand a chance. You might be turned into another creature like Slobbit!'

'I don't believe all that stuff about enchantment and transformation' cried Driftwood. 'Folk exaggerate — the story grows with the telling.'

Stumble shifted uneasily.

'You haven't drunk the pledge of loyalty, lad. I tell you whatever is working inside us is strange indeed. Whatever liquid it is that turns men to Dreirds must have enchantment about it. If it can enslave, why shouldn't it work other horrors as well?'

'Aye.' Strug agreed. 'Those cats of Fowler's — the hunting cats. I saw one down in Drocken Wood. Nigh as big as a leopard it was. And intelligent too. Men say it was an old peasant's cat. Fowler went into the peasant's house one day, and when he came out there was no sign of the old man or his cat. But this great black creature was walking by Fowler's side and rubbing itself against his leg.'

'The yarns people tell!' said Driftwood, his mouth full of bread and cheese.

'Maybe.' said Strug 'But the cat I saw was big I tell you. Tall as this table. It wasn't natural — I know that. No ordinary cat gets to that size and no ordinary cat looks at you the way that cat did!'

'Now,' said Stumble. 'We should reach Diamede in five days or so — it may take longer before we can persuade King Threld to grant us an audience. But within a fortnight we should be back and all be well again.'

'We'll close the business for a fortnight.' said Strug. 'You, Driftwood my lad, can take a fortnight's holiday. Go where you like but be careful to keep away from Fowler and the Dreirds. After all he doesn't know who you are, and once you're away from here there'll be naught to connect you with us.'

'After the fortnight you keep a watch on Black Tor.' Strug continued. 'When we get back we'll light this lantern and set it on top of the Tor each night. When you see that we're back, you can return secretly and we'll share our news. Hopefully all will be settled and life will go on again as before.'

'I'm really going to miss you.' said Driftwood.

'Aye lad, and we shall miss you too. But it won't be for long.'

Driftwood caught the expression on Stumble's face. It confirmed his own private thoughts. The plan sounded simple, but in fact the situation was desperate — and confused as well. There were too many unanswered questions. What if the two old men were clapped in a dungeon instead of being allowed to see King Threld?

He half opened his mouth to raise objections, but realised that it was pointless to say anything. All three of them understood the situation, but to encourage one another they would have to keep up the pretence that everything was going to be all right. He realised that he might not be bidding them a fortnight's farewell. He might be saying his last goodbye to the only people who had ever shown him love and protection.

Strug undid the canvas bag and shook out a great mound of gold coins.

'There's a time to save, and a time to spend.' he said.

'Driftwood, here are three coins for you. That should be plenty to last you a fortnight. Stumble and I will need money for our journey. The remainder we will return to its hiding place. If you run short, then come back by night and take another three, but be careful that you aren't seen! If for some reason we don't return. Then …' he swallowed hard, 'Well, lad, we've no one else to love. If we don't come back it's all yours. We trust that you'll be wise in the way you spend it.'

Stumble pushed his mug of soup away from him. It was untouched. For a moment Strug put his hands over his face. Then he pulled himself together and looked up.

'Fowler won't break us. Our wills are as stubborn as the rock we chisel. That's right, eh my brother? We'll speak to King Threld. That's what we'll do. We'll make him listen. But tonight I grow weary. Such a day we've had! Stumble you say the words'

They bowed their heads reverently and Stumble repeated the liturgy that they'd used each night for as long as Driftwood could remember.

'O thou the unknown who givest light. Give more light.'

Driftwood yawned as he repeated the words. When he looked up, Strug's head had fallen onto his arms which were resting on the table. Stumble bent over his brother, hesitated and decided not to wake him. Driftwood went to bed. Stumble picked up the lantern and went outside to check that that there were no Dreirds lurking in the shadows.

CHAPTER 3
DROCKENWOOD

*F*or the first time in his young life, Driftwood found that he couldn't sleep. He felt as if all the nerves in his body were jangling. He knew that he would feel better if he could doze off, but still he tossed and turned on his straw pallet. It felt prickly and uncomfortable and his brain was teeming with thoughts. What if Fowler had captured him! Would he ever see Strug and Stumble again? Then he thought about his own parents drowning in the storm.

To blot out his sad and troubling thoughts he concentrated on more pleasant ones. He had money to spend and was about to go exploring. It would be exciting. What would he need to take with him? He began to think about Strug's flick knife. He had always wanted a knife like that. So sharp and strong — the sinister click it made as it opened. How he would like a knife like that! Surely, now that he was going to be on his own he would need a weapon to protect himself with.

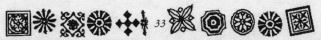

He thought of the three gold coins. There were shops down in Cragrock. It would be risky, but he knew an ironmonger's in a back street where he could buy a knife like Strug's. The trouble was that he had only enough money to buy food and shelter. Strug had never encouraged extravagance. There might be a little left over, but the knives were very expensive — another gold coin would make all the difference. Strug had said that he could help himself to three more when he needed them. Surely it would be better to take them straight away. But what about Strug who was still sleeping soundly at the table?

Before he had time to think any more, Driftwood was on his feet and creeping back into the shed. The gentle sound of Strug's snores filled the building. One of his hands was round the bag of coins, but the bag was open and a few had spilled out onto the table. Three would be enough. Strug and Stumble wouldn't notice, and anyhow they had said that it would all be his in the end. He reached out his hand and Strug stirred in his sleep. Hardly daring to move, Driftwood paused as the breathing became steady again. Once more he stretched out his hand towards the coins. Then suddenly he knew that he couldn't do it. His guardians had shown him love. It wasn't fair on them. He would be stealing. Sadly he crept back to bed. But even as he lay down, the ground under him shuddered and then a great stillness came into the room.

Never before had Driftwood been troubled by the terror of Black Tor. He lay in the darkness shaking with fear. All sorts of accusing thoughts came into his mind. He remembered times when he had lied to Strug or been cross with Stumble. He recalled conversations he had heard at the Tipsy Goose, jokes that he didn't fully understand, but which he knew were wrong. He reflected on the occasions when he had been selfish or cruel. But above all he was ashamed at the very thought of stealing from Strug.

'I don't understand it.' He thought to himself. 'I didn't even steal anything. I only thought about it. I didn't do it. Why should Black Tor be angry with me?'

But there was no doubt in his mind that Black Tor was angry. He was not experiencing the extremes of terror that had sent some villagers screaming from the slopes of the hill. But he felt bad enough. He stuffed the corner of the blanket into his mouth and gritted his teeth on it to stop himself from shouting out. He forced himself to keep still. It wasn't only fear of the unknown that had gripped him, but much more a sense of disgust and loathing of himself. He had never felt so miserable in his life. His thoughts focused on the storm that had washed him ashore — if only his parents hadn't drowned. He put one hand on the leather pouch in which the pearl was hidden and suddenly the terror had gone and he was sound asleep.

It was before dawn when Stumble woke Driftwood. The three had a hasty breakfast and spoke very little. Both old men looked worse than they had the night before. Driftwood wondered whether they would ever actually get to Diamede. But there was nothing he could do to help them and he knew that sympathy would be wasted.

'This is the plan we've got for you' said Strug. 'Our narrow gauge railway line runs down to Cragrock. Now Fowler's a stranger to these parts and we hope that he's unaware of it and of our mine. But as you know lad, the gradient is downhill all the way. The truck will gather speed even before it's out of the tunnel. Local people won't be surprised if the truck runs early. It's not the first time that we've taken dressed stones down to Cragrock.

Now you know where the track runs through Drocken Wood. When you get deep among the trees you must jump clear. It's not so steep there, and the truck will be slowing down. Leave it to run on into the siding. We'll bring it back when we return from Diamede.'

Driftwood said an unemotional goodbye and clambered into the truck. He knew that the old men had a deep love for him and were anxious about his safety. He also knew that he loved them. But it was a rare thing for any of them to show emotion. Indeed in the morning light their manner was more stern and unyielding than ever. Their faces were expressionless like the rock of Black Tor. It was as if something of the spirit of the mountain had entered their souls.

'Goodbye then' said Driftwood. 'I'll see you in a fortnight. The unknown attend you.'

Stumble put his shoulder behind the heavy truck and set it rolling downhill. It steadily gathered speed as its iron wheels rumbled and clattered over the rails. The walls of the tunnel shot past — the noise was terrific. Then the truck rattled through a cutting made between the rocks — the sound was deafening.

Still gathering speed, it hugged a bend with the cliff on one side, and a fearful drop on the other, then rushed on across barren moorland. Already in the distance Driftwood could see the dark line of the trees of Drocken Wood. The truck shot under the arch of a road bridge, then followed the line of the river for a few hundred metres. It began to slow down as it reached the shelter of the trees.

Driftwood had made this journey before and braced himself to jump. As the truck slowed on a bend, he flung himself out onto the springy turf and watched as the truck rumbled on down the track. He heard it clanking and banging as it picked up speed again. His last link with home had gone. He was on his own now.

In the fresh light of dawn it felt good to be alive. He didn't intend to squander his gold coins. He hoped he might find some work somewhere. Or maybe he would live like an outlaw. The great thing was to keep away from anyone who might identify him. He would be safe among strangers. He must keep clear of Dreirds and of Glummit's cronies who might recognise him.

After striding through Drocken Wood for some time, he came to a small clearing in the forest and found a pool of clear water. He hadn't washed his hands and face before breakfast, and stopped to do so. But as he looked into the pool, he stiffened with sudden fear. There, in the water was the reflection of a gleaming watchful eye. The huge cat was lying along the branch above him, its sleek body camouflaged by wood and dappled leaves. Perhaps it had been hoping for fish.

Driftwood flung himself sideways across the turf and, springing to his feet, ran for his life. The cat dropped exactly on the spot where Driftwood had been crouching. Had it not been for the speed with which Driftwood had moved, the slashing claws and sharp fangs would have been in his back. He got only as far as the middle of the clearing before the cat pounced. A fearsome blow from behind knocked him to the ground and as he looked up, his eyes met the merciless stare of the green eyed hunter.

'If only I had a weapon' he thought. 'Even a branch would help.' He tensed, waiting for the cat to spring. If he could just get among the trees he would be safe. Too late he realised that he should have made for the water. Retreat in that direction was now impossible.

'Nice pussy.' he said hopefully. 'Let's be friends eh?'

He reached out a cautious hand towards the creature. It responded with a sharp hiss of angry breath, like a red hot iron plunged into water. Driftwood froze; the cat waited. Out of the corner of his eye Driftwood spotted a fallen branch. Cautiously he got ready to make a dash towards it. The cat licked its lips. Taking that as a sign of loss of concentration, Driftwood sprang to his feet and ran like the wind.

With an effortless bound the cat reached him, but didn't scratch him at all. Suddenly Driftwood understood what was happening. Anger, humiliation, and horror swept over him in waves. He had become the creature's plaything. It would toy with him and allow him to escape again and again. Then in the end it would begin to use its claws and teeth. But how intelligent was it?

With another leap Driftwood reached the branch. He seized it as a weapon and, with fresh hope rising in him, swished it through the air at the cat. Momentarily the great animal backed away, spitting and hissing. Then, as Driftwood lunged at the animal, the branch suddenly split in two. Driftwood was horrified. For a moment he stood bemused, the broken stump in his hand. Then the absurdity of the situation struck him and he laughed. Flinging the stick away, he faced the monster and, although he wasn't sure if it would understand, he declared:

'I'm not a mouse; I'm a man. You may kill me. But I won't make sport for you. I'm not going to please you by running in fear. Claw me to death if you must. But you shall not rob me of my courage.'

'Bravely spoken, young Sir' said a voice behind him. 'But let me give you some better advice. It's too beautiful a morning to be talking of dying. Your day has just begun. Keep your eyes fixed on the creature and step back if you will — a pace at a time. That's the way. Easy now. Slow and steady. Don't take your eyes off him.'

Step by step, not daring to look round, Driftwood edged back, his every sinew taut as wire. He had cautiously withdrawn about four paces when everything suddenly happened. The cat leaped at him, slashing its extended claws towards his face and he was flung sideways by a shove on the shoulder. The cat shot past him and, unable to check its momentum, landed on the grass which immediately gave way. The animal plunged into a deep pit which had earlier been hidden by a net covered with branches and leaves — a neatly disguised trap. From far below came a furious screeching and miaowing as the cat tore at the overhanging sides of the pit in a vain attempt to escape.

Driftwood turned towards his rescuer — a short, stout elderly man who was holding out his hand in greeting. He wore a tweed jacket and trousers, a check shirt open at the sunburned neck and a green baize apron. On his head was a well worn cloth cap with a check pattern, and lodged behind his right ear was a yellow black-leaded carpenter's pencil. His silver grey hair was thick and curly and he boasted a splendid moustache. His cheeks were red like the apples of late autumn and his expression cheery and confident. His face was weather beaten, like that of a man who worked outside in all seasons. His eyes, under bushy silver eyebrows, were a strong blue, piercing and deep set, yet twinkling, with crinkled laughter lines around them. He looked as if he were still enjoying some joke.

'Well met, young Sir!' he declared dropping a leather bag on the ground with a thud and a rattle of tools. A distinct but not unpleasant whiff of linseed oil hung in the air.

'My name is Chuckle — Master carpenter, joiner boatbuilder and general handyman. At your service.'

'You saved my life!' said Driftwood simply.

'That's as maybe' grunted Chuckle, slightly embarrassed. 'Or if you'd rather, you could say like as how you helped me to trap him. I've been digging this pit in the hope of teaching that there cat a lesson. He's been a-hanging round the farm helping himself to livestock. Bill Arkwright's little girl had a narrow escape the other morning. Some say as how the cat belongs to a man called Fowler. You might have heard of him.'

'What will you do with it now you've caught it?' asked Driftwood.

'Arkwright owns this patch o'land. He'll get the constable up here, and they can take charge. I guess the Dreirds will come and collect him, but the disgrace will keep him out of mischief for a while. Fowler's cats aren't allowed to prey on farm animals.'

'It'd be better to kill it' said Driftwood indignantly.

'It's not a day for killing' replied Chuckle. 'I'm a carpenter, not an executioner. Come on young Sir, let's walk down to the town together. I've taken a liking to you. Tell me your name.'

Driftwood obliged and then asked cautiously. 'Have you had to take the pledge of loyalty?'

Chuckle shook his head. 'King Threld ruled wisely until that there Fowler turned up. I'm loyal to King Threld. Fowler doesn't turn everyone into Dreirds. Most people do their work and pay their taxes. For them, life goes on as usual.'

They took a path which led them down to the far side of Cragrock. It was a long way from the railway siding and in a different direction from the road to the Tipsy Goose. Driftwood felt confident that nobody would recognise him on this side of town. Soon he could smell the sea which told him that they were not

far from the harbour. As they walked, they chatted together.

Chuckle explained that he loved travelling. Sometimes he would be working in his shop, but more often he would set off with his bag, wander through towns and villages, do odd jobs here and there, listen to news of what was happening in the islands, and meet all sorts of interesting people. During the winter months he would turn his hand to building a small boat or two. By selling a dinghy he could make enough to set him off on his travels again.

Driftwood had never been in this part of the town before.

After a while they reached Chuckle's shop. It was nestled among other quaint and ancient buildings near the harbour wall.

CHAPTER 4
WATCHER IN THE SHADOWS

*C*huckle slipped a key into the lock and the bell above the door tinkled as they opened it. The bay window and door were glazed with panes of bullseye glass so that no one could see in. Driftwood guessed that the shop would look very cheery at night — like a lantern shining out into the street.

The ground floor was a single room. It had cupboards and a large workbench with an enormous vice. Tools hung on whitewashed walls; ropes, fishing nets and floats were suspended from wooden pegs. There was a smell of resinous wood, with a hint of paraffin, lavender and herbs. It was a pleasant workshop. There was no attempt at decoration. But perhaps because everything had a use, and was kept bright and shiny, it was an attractive place with a charm of its own.

'I sleep upstairs.' said Chuckle. 'My cooking's simple. Nothing fancy you understand. I do it on the stove over there in the corner.'

By this time they were both ready for lunch. Chuckle produced half a pie, some pickle, and strong tea in mugs. Driftwood had decided that he was completely trustworthy and bit by bit related his story — about life at Black Tor, Strug and Stumble, the gold and the shipwreck long ago.

'I'd like to see that there little pearl of yours' said Chuckle.

Driftwood fumbled in the leather pouch, and drew it out. Chuckle held it delicately between finger and thumb. Then he took it to the window where the strong sunlight shone in among the tools and shavings on his work bench. He undid a leather pocket in his carpenter's bag and took out a jeweller's glass which he fixed into his eye. Then he peered at the pearl again. Finally he grunted to himself as if satisfied.

'This was on you when you were washed ashore, you say?'

'That's right. I told you.'

'Did Fowler see this pearl?'

'Fowler didn't even see me, let alone the pearl.'

Chuckle turned from the window, removed the glass from his eye and looked long and steadily at Driftwood. Then he put a hand gently on his shoulder.

'I'm glad I met you this morning young Sir.'

'Is the pearl precious then?' asked Driftwood eagerly.

'You'll not be able to sell it if that's what you mean by precious. Anyways I don't think as how you do mean that. Yes, it's precious. Happen there aren't so many pearls like that in our world. Let me tell you, young Sir, that pearl is worth you a-holding onto. Never let that there Fowler know aught about your pearl, or how you came by it!'

'Fowler has no idea about me or where I am.' replied Driftwood confidently.

'Come over to the window' replied Chuckle. 'But keep back a bit.'

By peering out sideways through the window, Driftwood could see into the street without being seen himself.

It was quiet in the afternoon sunshine. Someone was looking at the paintings in the artist's window. A stout woman with a basket over her arm was chatting with the greengrocer as she bought some vegetables from his stall. A hopeful dog sat yawning in the shadows outside the butcher's. An occasional cart rattled slowly past over the cobbles, with the clip clop of horse's hooves.

'What am I supposed to be looking at?' whispered Driftwood.

'Wait a bit, young Sir, wait a bit.' admonished Chuckle. 'You must learn to wait and watch and wait again until you see.'

Still nothing seemed to happen. Perched on roofs and chimney pots gulls cried the news of fishing. The whole village seemed to be half asleep.

Then suddenly Driftwood saw what Chuckle wanted him to see. In an alleyway between two shops, there was a slight movement. A man, hooded and cloaked, was standing in the darkness. There was no doubt who it was. Driftwood backed away from the window and

tried to sound casual. He didn't want Chuckle to see him as a coward.

'Do you think he knows I'm here?' he asked.

'No' replied Chuckle. 'Fowler's been a-spying on me before. He suspects me of many things and not without some reason. But what he suspects is one thing, and what he knows is another. He'll not trouble us while it's day — but after dark, who can tell? He loves the night.'

'I'll escape by the back door.' suggested Driftwood.

'Aye — but let me see if the coast is clear first. You stay back from the window.'

Chuckle slid the bolts on the back door and stepped onto the gravel path with some rubbish for the dustbin at the bottom of the garden. Driftwood listened to the sounds of the seashore, the gentle foam and splash of the waves, the cries of the gulls and the slap of halliards against the masts of anchored vessels. Then he heard the scrunch of Chuckle's feet on the pathway as he returned to the house. He was whistling a happy tune — until he closed the door behind him. Then his usually cheerful mouth was serious and unsmiling.

'Slobbit's a-hiding in the bushes next door' he said. 'He's keeping well down, but I can scent him a mile off. If you go that way he'll not hurt you by day, but once he's on your track that nose of his will snuffle you out later. Slobbit's not very bright — but he can track anyone down.'

'What should we do?' pondered Driftwood.

'Wait a while' said Chuckle. 'I'll tell you all I know about this pearl. You're safe for the moment.'

He sat down by Driftwood with the tiny pearl lying on the bench between them.

'I've seen that pearl before.' Chuckle began. 'It belongs to the Master, he who is called Daylord. Its nature is a mystery that belongs to another world and another time. All that I can tell you is that it cost the Daylord great suffering to obtain it. There was a time when he plunged into the depths of the sea. For three days and nights, he was hidden in the deep oceans and folks say as how that he visited another world and another time.

Anyways, one thing's for certain, at the end of the three days he came back with a great shout of triumph — though his poor body bore the dreadful marks of torture. He brought with him pearls like this one — many of them much larger. They were the rewards of victory. I saw them myself, I did.' Chuckle paused for a moment as if lost in memories that were precious to him. Then he continued,

'Well, young Sir. There came a day when this pearl was entrusted to a man who was directed to take it to Diamede because it was needed there. He was told to hold fast till further instructions were given — the Daylord never gives commands until the right time. But the trouble was that the man who was chosen was wild and rebellious. He took the three pieces of gold that he had been given for the journey, but he stole other gold beside. That gold were burning a hole in his pocket as they say.

Instead of coming to Diamede he went off. 'Tis a mystery where he went, or what he got up to — except that there were rumours of his wanderings in many far countries. Some folks say as how he spent all the money and in the end was worse off than if he'd never had the handling of it. Then there was talk of a marriage, but I don't know the ins and outs of all that or what became of them after.'

'Do you suppose he was drowned at sea?' asked Driftwood.

Chuckle's face was grave.

'The Daylord would be sad if that were so, young Sir. But by my thinking, that might well be.'

'I've always believed my father and mother were drowned.' said Driftwood. 'But how do you know all these things?'

'Oh I travel far. There's work for a carpenter even in the palace of a King. A skilled dovetail here, a new drawer there, a delicate casket of cedar wood maybe, even fine carvings in the royal apartments. If you look at that little crest on my tools it says, "By royal appointment".'

He chuckled to himself.

'Sounds very grand, don't you think, young Sir. But of course there are many of us. The Daylord always has plenty of labourers working for him. You might meet my friend, Calm one day. He's one as works over here as well. Still the story about the pearl is true enough. You can take my word for it.'

'Do you think that my mother and father were trying to get to Diamede when they were drowned?'

Chuckle sighed. 'More than likely they was, young Sir. Anyways, that's how it begins to look, seeing as how you've got the pearl. Folks have always thought that as like as not the wreck took place in the wild ocean beyond Black Tor. Other ships have gone down there — their masts a-broken and their sides stove in with the wild surf pounding at them.' He shuddered at the thought.

'You say my father was wild and rebellious' said Driftwood thoughtfully.

'He may have changed before he died' said Chuckle.

'Do you think I take after him?' demanded Driftwood.

The older man gazed steadily down into his face. Driftwood's eyes didn't falter.

'Yes, young Sir, you're much like him. And when you met the hunting cat in the forest, I saw it then. "Chuckle" I says to myself, "who does that youngster remind you of?" He had a way with him he had. Bold and frank he were. Many loved him. But he loved danger, and he loved gold. I think he loved the Daylord too. But he was wilful. He couldn't see that sometimes love means a-doing what you're told to do.'

There was a long silence as Driftwood pondered what Chuckle had said. Then he stood up, picked up the pearl and put it into the leather pouch around his neck. He felt somehow that he was faced with an important decision — though he didn't fully understand it.

'I shall do what my father intended to do. I shall take this pearl to Diamede' he said.

Chuckle clapped him on the shoulder. 'Well done, young Sir! But be warned. There's no trusting of that Fowler. Rumours travel. I'm not the only one who knows these tales I've been a-telling you.'

Later in the afternoon Chuckle boiled a kettle and over tea and buttered crumpets, they discussed Driftwood's escape

'Once you gets to my boathouse down by the harbour wall, you'll be able to hide, and nobody will find you there. Never fear for that. Inside the boathouse there's a dinghy. I've been a-working on that dinghy for weeks now — off and on like..I'm a giving her to you. Made of good timber she is, and the sails are stout canvass.'

Chuckle spread out a small map on the table and gestured over it with a half eaten crumpet.

'This isn't what you'd call a real chart. Anyways, it'll give you the outline of the islands right enough. Keep within sight of the shore and inside the great rocks. There's a safe enough channel, never fear for that. Sail when the weather is fine, but when the sky gets a bit dark, and the wind starts a-blowing, then be sure you're in harbour somewheres.'

Driftwood drained his mug.

'While you've been talking, I've had an idea' he said.

'That rope on the wall, it looks strong.'

'That it is for sure, young Sir. Good and strong, though slender. You could climb a cliff with that rope if you was a-thinking of doing so.'

'Not a cliff' said Driftwood.

Chuckle looked at him for a moment, then suddenly perceived what was in Driftwood's mind. He slapped his thigh delightedly.

Slobbit watched from the undergrowth. Most of his life was spent like this — hidden away in corners, spying for Fowler. It bored him. He was sleepy. But fear of Fowler kept him at his task. He sucked his finger, pulling at the corner of his mouth, watching the house in the hope that someone was hidden there. If the boy was inside, Fowler would be pleased with Slobbit.

Chuckle came out of the house. A clothes basket on his arm, and a hank of new rope lying in the basket. There was nothing in this for Slobbit. He wasn't allowed to cause trouble unless Fowler gave him permission. In any case, he knew something of Chuckle the carpenter.

Slobbit yawned. He watched as Chuckle replaced his worn and weathered clothes line with a brand new one. It was strung from near the attic window down to a beam of timber fixed to the stone wall at the end of the garden. Chuckle used a ladder to fix the line, which ran through a large pulley. When he had secured it, he returned the ladder to the garden shed. Later he pegged out some clothes. A few shirts, mainly brightly coloured with check patterns. They fluttered in the breeze.

Slobbit's head felt heavy. He lowered it until his chin nestled on his spread six fingered paws. A butterfly clung to a twig a few feet from Slobbit's snout, but he was half asleep now and too bored to reach out for it. Yet, his great goggle eyes never relaxed their steady observation of the house. He was trained to watch and to go on watching. Fear of Fowler guaranteed that he would not fall asleep.

Inside the house Chuckle and Driftwood had agreed their plan of escape. Chuckle went over the map with

Driftwood until he was sure that the lad had grasped the general geography of the islands.

''Tis a fair sight to see is Diamede.' said Chuckle.

'There's this crag. All on its own it stands, jutting straight up out of the ocean. See it from a distance and you'd say that it was all a-part of the cliff like. But you get a bit closer where you can hear the surf a-roaring against the shore, and you'll see as how there's no way into that Castle but by the drawbridge. 'Twas once a fine Castle — so folks say — but since Fowler has been viceroy to King Threld, things have changed. Too much money spent on feasting and the dungeons, 'tis a shame to see as how some of that fine stonework has been allowed to crumble.'

'Have you ever worked there?' asked Driftwood.

'Never' replied Chuckle. ''Tis no place for an honest workman I tell you. Nothing but Dreirds, and them big cats a-howling and poor prisoners a-tortured in the dungeons I wouldn't wonder. Fowler did ask me to supply a pillory once. Soon after he first took over it was. "That's no job for a kind hearted man" says I. Sneered at me he did, but he left me be.'

They sat for a while longer and then towards dusk Chuckle went out with his basket and gathered in his washing. He pretended to know nothing of the baleful eyes hidden in the bushes.

Driftwood noticed that outside in the street, dusk was turning to night. He was restless, and a little sad. He wished he could stay with Chuckle. He felt safe and comforted when Chuckle was there. But he didn't want to get the old man into trouble. He knew it was best that he should be in hiding. Already he was going over the details of his escape in his mind.

Slobbit was suddenly alert. The back door of Chuckle's cottage was opening stealthily. Slobbit crouched, ready to leap out. Chuckle stood outside the back door. There was a sudden flare of a match, and a candle lantern began to cast a small circle of light. Slobbit saw that as well as the lantern, Chuckle was carrying a shovel and a most interesting looking box.

Slobbit heard the scrunch of Chuckle's shovel as it bit into the loose soil in the back yard. It took Chuckle some time to dig the hole deeply enough for his satisfaction. Eventually he lowered the chest into it, and then refilled the hole. He smoothed the earth carefully, and replaced the turf.

Slobbit's whole attention remained riveted upon what Chuckle was doing. Something valuable must be hidden in that box. Slobbit was sure of that. Fowler would be pleased. Slobbit must memorise the place where the hole was dug. Chuckle was covering it in with care and in the darkness it would not be easy to find it again. Slobbit knew that he would find it though. He would be able to sense where it was. He would snuffle it out. Slobbit would get that box.

At the moment when Chuckle had cautiously opened the back door, Driftwood reached out from the window ledge where he had been standing, and groped in the dark for the rope that was to be his way of escape from the house. Fortunately it was dark. Yet if Slobbit were to glance up, he might sense that something was dangling above him. So Chuckle, with box, lantern and noisy shovel, was busy making sure that Slobbit was too engrossed to notice what was going on.

Driftwood had borrowed an old pair of woollen mittens from Chuckle's drawer. They would save his hands some punishment. He swung out on to the rope, travelling hand over hand, swinging himself along. He knew that the hardest part of the climb was yet to come. Already his arms were beginning to ache. Beneath him he could see the circle of light on the ground and could hear the scrunch of the shovel. Hand over hand, he hauled himself along the rope. Although the air was cool, beads of perspiration broke out on his face and ran into his eyes. He was pulling himself upwards now. But the worst thing was that he had to control his breathing. Slobbit's hearing was sharp. The sound of breathless gasps from above would certainly make him look up. Grimly Driftwood edged on.

Now the mittens which had helped him along the first part of the rope were slipping and spoiling his grip. Precious seconds were lost as he tore each mitten off, using his teeth, whilst hanging on one aching arm. He was tiring. He felt strongly tempted to allow himself to drop to the ground and make a run for it, but one cry would be enough to alert Fowler — and Slobbit would soon catch him. He swung on in grim silence, brushing the sweat away with his sleeve.

If only he could utter a groan! His heart was pumping so loudly that it seemed to him that surely Slobbit must hear it. He could tell he was nearing the post. It was more and more of a direct vertical climb now. He managed to swing up and get a hold on the rope with his feet. He clung like a monkey on a branch, finding some relief for his aching muscles. Then with an agonised heave, he hauled himself up, and then up again, until at last he found the post at the bottom of the garden, and swung himself onto it.

New strength came with the elation of having reached safety without raising any alarm. Below in the garden, Chuckle was filling in the hole. As he patted and thudded the soil with the flat of his shovel, Driftwood swung himself over the wall, and dropped almost soundlessly onto the tufts of heather below.

CHAPTER 5
NO ORDINARY CARPENTER

F owler enjoyed the feeling of the dark about him. During the daylight hours he was strong, but night refreshed him. When the sun was up he would move secretively, choosing ways that were subtle and devious. But in the velvet night, he acted confidently and with a heart as black as the darkness, set on every kind of evil.

He reached out a white bony hand. He had long fingers, and on the knuckles there were hard lumps beneath the skin. His finger nails were long and tapered. Over the sinewy hand he pulled a glove of black leather, soft, supple, perfectly fitted. He wrapped the hood of his cloak about his sharp nose and his thin lipped and cruel mouth. With the utmost caution he stepped out into the street.

From under his cloak he produced the materials he had prepared: old rags, shredded into streamers. There was a sudden stench of oil as Fowler soaked these,

pushing them hurriedly but silently through the letter box of Chuckle's shop. Finally, and less cautiously, he shook the rest of the contents of the bottle of oil inside the door.

Suddenly a match flared, and a moment or two later flames were leaping up inside the door. Fowler had already gone, lurking again where no one would see him or suspect what he had done.

Within a few minutes the shop was ablaze. The flames began to roar and crackle. Windows along the street were flung open. Heads began to peer out. A cry of alarm spread down the lanes. Before long people were running, calling for the Fire Brigade. Fowler knew about the local Fire Brigade — one old man, and a boy — both of them willing, but relatively unskilled. In an emergency, neighbours volunteered their help.

The fire appliance was a large barrel mounted on a handcart and a hand operated pump. For years the villagers had grumbled about it — but fires were few and the town council short of money. It would be some time before the fire was brought under control.

Chuckle would be forced to escape and if there was a boy inside, as Fowler suspected, then he would be driven out as well — or be burned alive. Fowler anticipated that the boy would run out into the back garden where Slobbit was waiting to pounce — Slobbit with his great thick six fingered paws, so strong that he could bend an iron bar. Slobbit would be waiting and he knew what to do. Fowler had forbidden him to kill the boy if he was there, but he must be brought to submit. One way or another Fowler had plans to use the boy. The old carpenter was disposable. He must be taught a lesson at last.

The cottage was blazing now — flames breaking through the thatched roof. The village was in an uproar.

Driftwood had travelled some distance by feeling his way along the dry stone walls at the backs of the houses. Now he was near enough to the harbour to see the occasional flash of light from the lighthouse on the headland, and the lighted cabins of one or two vessels lying at anchor in the pool. He could also scent the fresh tang of seaweed, and hear the rush and gurgle of gentle waves. The sea seemed drowsy and half asleep.

By now Chuckle's cottage was blazing like a torch, throwing the roofs of nearby houses into sharp relief. Lights were flashing everywhere; people were running and shouting. There was enough light for Driftwood to see the path more clearly so instead of creeping he was able to run. And run he did, till his breath came in gasps and his lungs were bursting. On he ran, keeping to the shadows, until at last he reached the shelter of Chuckle's boathouse.

Fumbling with an unfastened padlock and a creaking door, he took refuge in the shed. All sorts of smells mingled in his nostrils: creosote and tar, putty, varnish, and turpentine. Fishing nets festooned the walls. Sharp tools glinted in the lurid glow of the fire as they hung from racks fixed to the wall of the shed. Driftwood felt certain that Fowler would not be able to track him down. He hadn't touched the ground in the garden, so there was no obvious scent for Slobbit to follow. It would take Fowler some time to discover that he hadn't died, trapped in the inferno that blazed where Chuckle's cottage had stood for so many years.

Driftwood felt angry and upset. It was because of him that the fire had been started. The local Constable might think that it had been an accident, but Driftwood knew instinctively that it must be Fowler's work. Fowler was ruthless and implacable. The very suspicion that Chuckle was sheltering Driftwood had been enough to put the old man's life in danger. Chuckle had a right to live in his own cottage. It had been his business and his secure home, a place of welcome and hospitality for many. But now it was a stark outline on the harbour wall with flames pouring through the roof timbers and sparks soaring upwards into the night sky.

'If that's the punishment for sheltering me for a few hours, I hardly dare to seek protection from anyone again' thought Driftwood.

He remembered Strug and Stumble with their agonised faces. They too were suffering because they had tried to protect him. Suddenly he felt very tired and a wave of homesickness and sadness swept over him. He thought he would never fall asleep, but soon after he'd laid his head on a pile of netting on the floor, he was off into a dreamless slumber.

It was well that there was no one to observe Chuckle's movements as he returned from his pretence of hiding treasure in the garden. No doubt within a day or two Slobbit would retrieve the mysterious chest. He would have difficulty in opening it, for the brasswork and padlock were strong. When at last he did so, he would discover an old red velvet cushion in the middle of which was a very dry bone. Chuckle didn't think that Slobbit would appreciate the joke, but Fowler with cold sardonic humour would at least understand how and why Slobbit had been fooled.

The method of escape had been entirely Driftwood's idea. Chuckle had fallen in with the plan because wherever possible he liked young people to think for themselves and to show initiative. He rarely interfered. Had Driftwood asked for advice, Chuckle could have shown him an easier way to escape. There was a trapdoor, concealed in the floor of the cottage. It led into a dark tunnel and then out to the shore. Years ago the cottage had been used for smuggling and there were stories of adventure and sudden death.

Had Chuckle been an ordinary carpenter, he would have raised the trapdoor and escaped the fire that way. But he wasn't an ordinary carpenter. When alone he was free to act in the full power of another place and another time.

He opened a cupboard. Inside there stood a large and beautifully carved rocking horse. Its nostrils were touched with scarlet paint and the tips of its eyelids and eyebrows were ornamented with gold leaf. Fine ivory teeth showed in a fixed smile, as though the horse were eager to be off. It's mane and tail were of deep brown chestnut coloured hair, soft and flowing. The horse itself was white with black patches and the saddle and harness were of finest red leather. The metal of the harness was so bright that it could have been finely polished silver.

Chuckle made no attempt to stamp out the flaming rags that Fowler pushed through the door. Instead he went unhurriedly to a small cupboard and took out an ancient flask. Uncorking this, he poured the liquid carefully into a basin, which he held close to the horse's mouth and flared, carved nostrils. The first movement of life from the horse was a roll of the black painted eyeballs. They became living and bright as they moved. Gently, the horse lowered its nose. The snapdragon glow from the bowl in Chuckle's hand gave the white of the horses' head, a blue reflection. Now the horse was drinking eagerly. Blue flame was splashing over the sides of the bowl, bursting in a thousand twinkling points of light before it reached the floor.

The burning rags had done their work well; fire was spreading from the doorway.

''Tis time to be a going my beauty' said Chuckle.

He patted the horse gently on the head, and mounted the saddle. The rockers creaked once, twice, three times on the floor. Each plunge forward and sweep backward was greater than the one before. The yellow flames of the fire in the cottage flared up, the room was full of smoke but the living hooves of Fireflame had smashed clear of the rockers and now clattered upon a different road in another time and another place.

For a brief moment Chuckle saw far below him the burning cottage and the deeps of ocean beyond the harbour. But all was misty and unreal, for he was riding upon a surer path and a better highway, where even the stars themselves were no more than shiny pebbles as they twinkled beneath his horse's hooves. For Chuckle was no ordinary carpenter — he journeyed by another road and in another way.

Driftwood woke to the noise of gulls crying and shrieking on the roof above his head. Sunlight streamed through the window and lit up the fresh, clear varnished timbers of a sailing dinghy. The varnish was dry, yet so smoothly applied that the grain of the wood was clear and seemed almost wet, as a shiny pebble looks when it's taken from a rock pool. Painted on the stern in graceful script was the name, 'Driftwood.'

'Strange!' thought Driftwood 'Why did he use that name? Perhaps it was just a coincidence. Yet I wonder ...'

Tiller and rudder were already in place. Oars, as fresh as the boat itself, lay neatly across the foredeck and thwart. A strong canvas bag contained bright scarlet sails, and the mast, gaff and boom were all ready. Driftwood felt tears in the corner of his eyes and hastily brushed them away. He thought he had never seen anything quite as beautiful as this boat with its curving timbers, neat copper nails and shiny brass fittings.

'I do hope Chuckle escaped that fire' he thought to himself.

Chuckle's shed must have housed much bigger vessels in the past. There was plenty of room for Driftwood to rig the boat completely before he opened the great double doors. He rigged the boat very carefully, checking and double checking, adjusting the forestay and shrouds, testing the halliards. He wanted to be sure that nothing would get tangled or caught up. His experience of sailing was limited to a few fishing trips with cronies from the Tipsy Goose. This dinghy was smaller than theirs, but the principles were the same and Driftwood was bright enough to work things out for himself.

He knew that his life depended upon a smooth escape. There must be no fumbling about in full view of the village. Hopefully Fowler would think that he had been burned when Chuckle's cottage went up in flames. Provided he didn't attract attention, nobody would take much notice of a small boat out at sea.

Conditions were ideal. Driftwood peeped through the window of the shed. The sea was calm, the wind gentle. The sun sparkled on the water and in the distance grey cliffs met a sea as blue as sapphire.

He sat on a coil of rope and carefully thought out every move. It was still very early in the morning. After the excitement of the night, the village seemed asleep. Wet, charred and blackened timbers were all that remained of Chuckle's cottage.

Driftwood tested the bolts of the double doors that faced seawards. They were well oiled and would move easily. He checked the dinghy once more, then eased the bolts down and gently pushed the doors open. The sunlight and fresh sea air transformed the shed. He propped timbers against the doors to prevent them swinging shut, then began to push the dinghy on to the rollers.

He tried to be quiet, but it was impossible to prevent the rollers from rumbling. Deciding that speed was essential, he pushed harder. Down the ramp the boat bumped and rattled. As the bow plunged into the water, Driftwood flung himself aboard over the stern. The next few moments were busy. He hauled up the main halliard, then the jib, and grabbed for the sheets and tiller as he lowered the centreboard. The little pennant flew out from the masthead, the boom swung over and the mainsail filled with wind. It was a clumsy departure but 'Driftwood' was on her way. The water gurgled and bubbled under her bows. The wake lengthened behind her stern and she heeled slightly in the breeze.

CHAPTER 6
NEARSTRAND

*A*ll that morning Driftwood held to his course. He varied it a little as he became more confident as a helmsman — putting further out to sea, and then 'going about' and following the coastline more closely. He was careful to keep within eyesight of the shore. He had no compass and knew that he couldn't afford to take risks.

As the afternoon wore on, he began to feel very hungry and tired — he hadn't eaten any breakfast. Ahead of him lay an island which Chuckle's map had identified as Nearstrand. He could see a bay of white sand and a wooden quay jutting out from the shore. The three gold coins were a generous allowance of money and in the circumstances he saw no reason why he shouldn't spend some time on the island.

He reckoned that he'd sailed far enough away from Fowler. There was little risk of anyone taking much notice of him here. However, since his boat was small,

he didn't land at the quay, but instead found a secluded spot along the shore. He dragged the dinghy above the high water mark and having stowed away the sails, he hid the boat as well as possible before leaving the beach in search of food and shelter.

The road he took from the beach wasn't much more than a sandy cart track. He passed a few cottages and then found a larger farmhouse standing isolated from the others. As he approached it he could see a painted board hung from a post in the front garden.

DUNROAMIN
Bed and Breakfast
Proprietor H. Humple Esq.

The house seemed harmless and homely. Driftwood climbed the white steps and banged on the door. After a pause, there was the sound of footsteps, the rattling of bolts and then the clank of a chain. Finally the door opened. Inside stood a stout, somewhat rotund individual. He was balding and double chinned. He eyed Driftwood affably enough, although his smile was not very attractive.

'Can you give me supper and a bed for the night?' asked Driftwood politely.

'Indeed, indeed, come in and welcome' replied the man who was almost bowing in his eagerness to show deference to his young visitor. 'I will call my dear wife' he went on 'My name, young gentleman, is Humple. Er Herbert Humple. Herbert Humple Esq., at your service at all times." He raised his voice slightly.

'Hazy my dear, my beloved, we have a visitor, a paying guest.'

Driftwood noticed that Herbert licked his lips before he said 'paying'. Hazy Humple appeared from the kitchen, drying her hands on her apron. She was much taller than her husband, somewhat muscular with a sallow rather unhealthy looking complexion.

Hazy and Herbert showed Driftwood straight upstairs to his bedroom. Everything was scrupulously clean and neat. Nothing was out of place. All the wallpaper was new, and the paintwork was clean and fresh. Yet it wasn't really a welcoming atmosphere. The furniture was heavy and old fashioned, the air a little damp and chilly. There was a kind of deadness in the atmosphere as though the room itself was saying, 'Don't stay too long.' Driftwood shivered a little. The affable Herbert Humple Esq., stood in the middle of the room smirking and rubbing his slightly sweaty palms together.

'Just one thing, my dear young Sir — no offence I'm sure, but it's payment in advance if you don't mind. I'm sure you understand. Times are hard. The price of food is always going up, and being on an island makes shopping more expensive. Then, ahem, and once again most humbly begging your pardon, but there is the little matter of your luggage. You seem to have mislaid it. Not of course that it's important. We can supply towels for a small extra charge and we can sell you a toothbrush, soap ...' he paused as if struggling with himself, ' ... soap is provided' he added with a burst of generosity.

'You are not offended I trust young Sir, our only desire is to have a good understanding from the very

beginning. Hazy and I have been unfortunate, very unfortunate. Yes, I fear my dear Hazy is altogether too trusting. I have frequently said to her, "Hazy my dear, my beloved, your good nature will be your downfall. You are too trusting, Hazy. Altogether too trusting. Isn't that what I say, Hazy?"' Hazy opened her mouth and spoke for the first time.

'You do, Humple, you do.'

Driftwood eyed the trusting Hazy with mild surprise. Her voice positively boomed out. It was loud and deep — like a foghorn. Her expression was grim and there were lines round her hard mouth. To look at her no one would have guessed that there was a guileless spirit within. Driftwood wondered how sincere Herbert was in his praise. But he was still talking.

'Yes, my dear young gentleman. Payment in advance if you don't mind. Otherwise my sweet Hazy might go to all the trouble of cooking a delicious supper, and we might put you to sleep in our lovely clean white sheets — which Hazy washes with her own precious fingers — not to mention the expense of the soap. And then ...' A harsh suspicious note crept into Herbert's voice, 'and then you might tell us you had no money after all. Bah! No money! That was the trick Sorrel played on my poor trusting Hazy. Do I not tell the truth, Hazy?'

'You do, Humple, you do!' bellowed Hazy. A small fleck of whitewash floated down from the plastered ceiling. Hazy seemed to address her husband as though he were deaf, or several fields away. Driftwood winced slightly, fumbled in his jacket and produced a gold piece. His pride was a little hurt. He presented the coin with something of a flourish.

'Aah!' Herbert sighed with satisfaction and bobbed and bowed. His eyes glinted eagerly as he took the coin and carefully counted out the change. Hazy almost curtseyed in her satisfaction and hurried out of the room to prepare the supper. Driftwood decided he would eat in the bedroom and asked whether he could have a fire since the room felt chilly.

Driftwood could hear Hazy's voice booming in the distance. She was bawling at someone in the kitchen. The house was quite large. Even bigger than it seemed from the outside. To begin with it had probably been a farmhouse. But there was no sign of farm machinery or animals now.

Within a few minutes Herbert Humple returned armed with coals and wood to make a fire. Behind him came a girl of about Driftwood's age. She might have been pretty, but her face was pinched and hungry looking, her hair was scragged back untidily and her clothes didn't fit her well. Her hands were rough with housework. She was carrying a brass warming pan with a long wooden handle. While she used this to warm the sheets, Herbert nagged at her incessantly.

'Hurry up Sorrel. Don't scorch the sheets. The young gentleman is tired after his journey. Mrs Humple will be in a hurry for you to bring up the tray. I was telling the young gentleman about you, Sorrel. How you took advantage of my poor trusting Hazy. It's a very wicked thing not to pay your debts, Sorrel. Al-

most as wicked as gambling your money away, instead
of putting it in a nice safe place. But we shall improve
you, never fear. We shall certainly improve you. My
dear Hazy will improve you. You'll be very grateful to
us in the end, even though your attitude is not yet what
it should be, if I may say so. You will know the value
of money by the time my dear Hazy has improved you.
You won't ever want to play dice or cards, or go to the
arcade again.'

Driftwood felt quite indignant. There was no need
for Humple to go on at the girl like this. The man just
didn't seem to be able to stop talking. He felt sorry for
Sorrel. Her face was hidden from him, but her neck
looked pink with shame or anger, or perhaps both. He
wondered how much of this he could stick before he
booted the kneeling Humple into his own grate. But at
that moment the fire began to crackle in the wood, and
Humple, having made good use of the heavy iron tongs
to pile the coal in place, left the room. Sorrel followed
him.

Driftwood used the ewer and handbasin for a thor-
ough wash and brush up. Periodic bursts of bawling
and bellowing came from the kitchen where Hazy was
presumably improving Sorrel. Driftwood dressed again,
and was tidying away the towel when there was a
knock on the door and Sorrel entered with the supper
tray. She didn't even glance at Driftwood, but putting
the tray on the bedside table, hurried from the room.

He wondered what the supper would be like. Somewhat to his surprise it was excellent: sausages, chips,
tomatoes, eggs, mushrooms — even a succulent piece

of steak and two rashers of bacon. He was ravenous, and ate away contentedly. The Humples were obviously keen to encourage him to prolong his stay. Nothing had been neglected. Later Herbert returned to take away the plates, and bring a dish full of delicious apple pie. There was nothing wrong with Hazy's pastry either — unless Sorrel had cooked the meal.

Gradually Driftwood was beginning to feel differently about Dunroamin. Maybe it was a good place after all. Perhaps he would stay for a week or two. The price was about average and his money would last for a long while. For the first time, all seemed comfortable and he gazed happily into the glowing coals of the fire, listening to the dry rustle and crackle as the red coals shifted and the yellow flames danced. Life here was not going to be so bad after all.

He was almost drowsing off to sleep when Sorrel knocked at the door again, bringing with her a silver tray with a coffee cup, and jug, a bowl of brown sugar, and a chocolate mint. The bone china cup had a paper doily between it and the saucer. Sorrel put the tray on a table by Driftwood's chair next to the fire, collected the other supper things and left the room without a glance or a word.

With a sigh of satisfaction, Driftwood leant forward to pour his coffee. But as he lifted the delicate cup from its saucer, he saw that there was a message written on the doily — just two words printed clearly: 'Don't drink.' Crumpling the doily thoughtfully, he tossed it into the fire then cautiously raised the cup to his lips and sniffed at its contents. It smelt like coffee, but not quite like coffee — just a little too bitter. He put down the cup, went to the bedroom door and tried the handle. It was a heavy door, in keeping with the rest of the farmhouse, and it was locked from the outside. Sorrel hadn't locked it when she left — he was sure of that. Someone had crept up the stairs in the dark and had stealthily turned the key. The lock must be very well oiled to make no sound.

'What kind of a place is this?' he asked himself as he sat down on the bed and put his head between his hands.

Later he arranged a bolster in the bed to make it look as though someone was asleep under the blanket. Then he went to the fireplace and picked up the long iron poker. Smiling grimly to himself, he pushed the end of the poker in among the red hot coals and went over to the window. There were iron bars outside. Sitting in a corner of the room next to the fireplace, he rested his head against the wall and began to keep watch on the door.

The house had become very quiet and still. A clock in the hall below struck eleven. Driftwood was sleepy and the room was warm. But the sense of danger kept him alert. Time passed. The clock struck midnight. A few minutes later he heard the sound of stealthy movements from outside the door.

There was the faintest click as the well oiled lock responded to the key. The door opened slowly without so much as a creak and the fire gave off enough light to throw a grotesque shadow on the wall. Hazy Humple was creeping towards the bed with an enormous meat chopper raised above her. Behind her tip toed Herbert with a finger stuffed into each ear.

With one lithe movement, Driftwood jumped from his hiding place and snatched his weapon from the fire. The tip of the long poker was white hot. With a jeer of triumph Driftwood waved it like a sword in their faces. He knew that there would be no real fight as he drove them back into a corner and away from the door. Then, still brandishing the poker, he leapt outside the door and turned the key in the lock. The pair were trapped in their own prison!

'Fool, Humple, Fool' bawled Hazy. 'How are we to get out without damaging the paintwork!'

Without waiting to hear more, Driftwood hurried down the stairs and into the kitchen where he found Sorrel with a gag in her mouth, tied to an old kitchen chair in front of a large wooden table. He removed the gag and quickly slashed the ropes with a carving knife.

'I'm so glad you found my note!' she said. Her voice was pleasant, but crisp and matter of fact. 'I didn't dare say anything when I brought the tray. Herbie was hiding just outside the door. I was afraid you might not read it until you'd downed the potion. They wanted your gold you see and tied me up for fear that I would warn you. But for once I got the better of them. I heard them plotting when I was out of the room getting the apples for the pie. I knew they were horrid, but I never believed that they'd try to murder anyone. It was seeing all that gold. It was so much money! You must be very rich.'

Driftwood wasted no time in talking. He cut through the last rope and she stood up, rubbing her cramped limbs.

'Come on!' he cried. 'They'll be out of there before long. Let's get going.'

'You'll take me with you then?' she asked eagerly.

'Of course. You didn't think I'd leave you with those two monsters, did you? But there's no time to waste.'

Feet pounding on the gravel they ran down the cart track that led to the beach.

'Have you ever been night sailing?' Driftwood panted.

'Never' she replied.

'Neither have I, but there's a first time for everything. We'll row to begin with. Give me a hand to get this boat launched.'

'We'll be all right' said Sorrel confidently as they leaped aboard and pushed out to sea. 'You can't miss the lights of Heartsease.'

'Where's that?' asked Driftwood bending his back to the oars. She pointed over his shoulder and turning he saw a blaze of coloured lights tucked into a fold of the hills. The rest of the dark mass of land was hard to distinguish from the cloudy sky above it. But although it was the middle of the night, the bay gleamed and glittered across the water.

'Even I should be able to find that in the dark' said Driftwood.

A little to his chagrin, he soon discovered that Sorrel was much more familiar with boats than he was.

She had lived on the island for a long while and was used to the ways of the sea. Before long the sails were hoisted, and with Sorrel at the tiller and Driftwood leaning out over the side, the dinghy was creaming through the gentle waves towards the brilliance that shimmered over the water on a pathway of twinkling colours.

CHAPTER 7
'WANTED'

'*I*'ve only heard rumours about Heartsease' said Driftwood. 'It sounds a nice place, but do you know what it's really like?'

'I know it like the back of my hand' said Sorrel confidently.

'There's a poor district and some crime. You have to be careful. But so long as you've got the money, there's all the fun you could ever want — and there's plenty of money about — all because of Potlot.'

'What on earth do you mean "Potlot"?'

'Fowler's Pharmaceuticals' explained Sorrel. 'Chemicals and beauty preparations — all that sort of thing. People began by calling it "Potions and Lotions," so it became "Potlot". That's much easier to say than "Pharmaceuticals". It's a great set of buildings out on the hillside above the town and it's linked with the quartz mines.'

'If Fowler has anything to do with Heartsease, I'm not going near the place' declared Driftwood firmly.

'Please yourself' replied Sorrel. 'But at the moment we don't have much choice. Neither of us knows the rest of the coastline and there are bound to be rocks under the water. It's pitch black up against the shore. Unless we make for the lights we'll probably smash your boat up. Besides why are you so worried about Fowler. You haven't met him have you?'

'No,' said Driftwood. 'But he turned some of my friends into Dreirds and my guardians are going to complain to King Threld about him. He's searching for me, even though he doesn't know what I look like.'

'We'd better be careful then.' replied Sorrel.

'It looks as if we're both on the run. The Humples will be after me, and Fowler after you. There are quite a lot of Dreirds about in Heartsease. They supervise the quartz mine and keep order in the town. The trouble is that apart from that green breath of theirs, they look like everyone else, and you can't see their breath in the daylight.'

By this time they were near enough to the bay of Heartsease to be able to see the lights more clearly. A brightly illuminated pier stretched out into the water and all around the bay, the roads and walkways were hung with brilliant coloured lanterns. It was a different world to anything Driftwood had ever seen and to him it looked like a great city.

Beyond the waterside lay the bay on which the town was built. The houses were amazing. The town glowed like a fire — because the buildings were not made of stone but of translucent quartz. Houses, shops and buildings of all kinds covered the terraces on the hillside. No two were quite the same and in the darkness they shone like ornamental lanterns. Driftwood was amazed. Life at Black Tor had never been like this. Even the Tipsy Goose seemed a drab little place compared to these brilliant streets and blazing houses.

'Doesn't anyone ever go to bed?' he asked in astonishment, as the distant sound of music drifted to them across the calm water of the bay.

'Oh yes,' replied Sorrel carelessly 'Towards morning they begin to switch off the lights. But they stay up till all hours. I used to enjoy it no end — when I was in the money that is.'

'Did you live here then?'

Sorrel sighed. 'I really lived in the poor part of town, but the old nurse who looked after me died just before my tenth birthday. She left me a bit of money and I made a few friends in the expensive part of town. Sometimes I stayed in their houses for weekends. It was fun while the money lasted, but once I lost my money I lost my friends. Where are we going to beach the boat?'

'As far away from the lights as possible. I don't want to get arrested by the Dreirds.'

Finding a little inlet at one corner of the bay away from the lights, they dragged the dinghy over the sand, stowed everything neatly and hid it in the dunes. Then they carefully memorised the spot so that they would be able to find it again and set off through the sand and grasses till they found a track leading away from the beach. By this time the lights were going out and the first light of dawn was appearing. Both of them were struggling with sleep and eventually sat down to rest.

'We're safer here than in the town' said Driftwood. 'Let's take a nap. We'll be able to see our way soon.'

When they woke up they were both tired, and longing for breakfast.

'At least we've got money' said Driftwood.

'Yes, but don't flash it around.' said Sorrel.

'How are we to explain that we're together?' she went on thoughtfully. 'I know, we'll say that we're brother and sister.'

'That's not true.' objected Driftwood. 'My guardians taught me never to tell lies.'

'How very inconvenient,' said Sorrel. 'I've had a lot of practice at telling lies. You'd better let me do the talking. But anyway ...' she added with a ripple of laughter, 'you can't prove I'm not your sister. You don't know who your parents were and I don't know who my parents were either — so why don't we adopt each other?'

'Good idea' agreed Driftwood. 'But if you're going to be my sister, you're going to have to stop telling lies.'

'Right,' said Sorrel cheerfully.

'I'll start telling the truth straight away — you're a pain in the neck!' She ran ahead laughing and Driftwood chased after her.

The sandy track led upwards into sparse woodland where there were pine needles under their feet. Beyond that there was a gravel path which led to the very outskirts of the town. The first building they came to was no more than a roadmender's shed.

'Look at this' cried Sorrel.

Pasted to the door was a fresh poster.

'Wanted. Information leading to the capture of a boy named Driftwood. Guilty of hooliganism at the Tipsy Goose, Black Tor. Reward £5.'

'Hooligan eh!' Sorrel grinned.

'£5 is a bit on the cheap side' complained Driftwood.

Sorrel put her head sideways, weighing him up.

'£3 maybe' she decided.

'Anyway, there's no description. You'll have to change your name.'

'I could call myself Herbert Humple Esq.' suggested Driftwood. Sorrel made a face at him.

Although they put a brave face on it, both felt more nervous now. There was less laughter and by mutual consent they edged higher up into the forest, rather than down the road into Heartsease. To their surprise they found that over the crest of the hill there was another secluded bay. The cliffs were granite and ran down steeply to the water. Only one craft was in the bay and it was a vessel unlike anything that Driftwood had ever seen before.

At the bows a great prow rose high above the water and the very top was skilfully carved into the likeness of the face of a lion. The vessel had three masts, and amidships a large cabin or deckhouse structure. The stern rose gracefully to match the prow. The craft seemed designed primarily for rowing. It looked as though it might have been shaped on the pattern of some ancient vessel used by marauding pirates. However at present it was under repair, for although it was still early in the morning, the noise of hammering and sawing came up in the still air.

'So that's where they went with it' exclaimed Sorrel.

'Who do you mean?'

'Oh, a queer bunch of people. Quite friendly they were, but different somehow. Nobody in Heartsease liked them much.'

Sorrel continued to talk as they walked on through the trees and away from the bay, taking a grassy path that led downhill.

'These ship people — they follow the old legends.'

'What legends?'

'Oh you know ... stories about invisible powers of light and darkness, and about fighting them with glittering shields. Then there's that song about the pearl bearer and the four carpenters — you must know that one!"

'No, I don't know. Tell me' said Driftwood eagerly.

'Its only a load of rubbish — a bit boring really. They made us learn some of the ballads at primary school. There was one about a pearl diver called Daylord. Then there was this carpenter's song. I used to enjoy it because of the music. It was a jolly good tune. I can't remember the words except when the music goes up at the end. I liked that bit.' She began to sing.

'Umpty umpty umpty umpty, dah de dah de dah,

umpty umpty umpty umpty. Four Carpenters to fray.'

Her voice was quite good, and Driftwood sensed that it was a fine tune. But being a boy he pretended to be in agony, and stuffed his fingers in his ears.

'Umpty umpty dah de dah' he said scornfully. 'What kind of a song is that.'

'I told you,' she replied a little huffily. 'I can't remember any of the words, only the last bit. But it's a jolly good tune!'

'Tell me some more about the legends' Driftwood begged.

But Sorrel had lost interest in the whole thing. She was a bit piqued by his criticism of her singing, and even though she knew it was a joke, she went quiet for a time. Both of them were feeling more and more hungry and could easily have had a quarrel. But fortunately they suddenly came upon a small cottage with a thatched roof.

CHAPTER 8
DOVE COTTAGE

*T*he cottage was set in a bowl in the hillside and could easily be passed by without anyone seeing it — although it could be approached from the other side by a small country lane. Steps led down from an iron front gate. There were masses of flowers on the banks of the sunken garden and the scent of herbs was strong.

The leaded lights of the windows sparkled in the fresh light of morning and goldfish swam in a small pool in the garden. The whole place seemed friendly and inviting. An elderly lady was stooping over a flower bed near the front gate. When she caught sight of them looking in, she straightened to speak to them.

'What beautiful flowers!' began Sorrel tactfully.

The old lady looked back at her with keen eyes that twinkled behind her spectacles.

'And what empty tummies!' she replied, as if they were her welcome grandchildren whom she had known

all her life. 'Come straight in, the kettle's almost boiling. I came out to wait for you — I wondered where you'd got to.'

Driftwood and Sorrel glanced at each other. They were amazed at this kind of welcome from a stranger.

'There must be some mistake' faltered Driftwood.

'You don't know us. My name is ...' he stopped, suddenly realising that he must either give a false name, or risk everything.

'Hello. I'm Beryl, and this is my brother Albert' said Sorrel cheerfully holding out her hand in greeting. 'We'd be ever so grateful if you could give us something to eat. We're on a walking holiday together and we've lost our way.'

'Of course I'll give you something to eat, Sorrel' replied the old lady. 'And Driftwood, do put that money away. You'll need it later on. Now come along in, both of you. First of all, a good wash and tidy up. You'll find everything you need in the bathroom. Driftwood yours is the blue toothbrush, and pink for Sorrel. I've laid out towels and flannels. By the time you're clean and tidy, breakfast will be served. Do you like eggs and bacon?'

She swept them before her, like a mother hen rounding up her chicks. It was extraordinary. Neither of them had ever known a welcome like this. It was as if everything had been prepared in advance.

The cottage was a place of sunshine, flowers and the fragrance of lavender. It had comfortable furniture, cosy cushions, highly polished tables, shelves of books, porcelain figurines, a carriage clock on the mantelpiece and an arrangement of dried flowers in the grate. From the kitchen came the aroma of coffee percolating and the hiss and crackle of frying bacon.

Driftwood and Sorrel, both of them tidier and cleaner than they had been for some time, slipped into the places prepared for them. The table cloth was starched white, the silverware sparkled and fresh flowers stood in a vase in the middle of the table. Sorrel looked around, wide eyed and breathed a sigh of satisfaction.

'Do you think it's a trap?' whispered Driftwood uneasily.

Before Sorrel could reply the old lady came through from the kitchen.

'Now my dears, enjoy a good breakfast' she said cheerily. 'Fruit juice and cereals on the trolley. Help yourselves. Milk in the jug. There's plenty of everything — and don't be frightened. You're safe here. No one will harm you or give any secrets away.'

'It's as if she can read our thoughts' murmured Sorrel. 'Do you suppose she's a witch?'

'Don't say that.' pleaded Driftwood. 'If she knows everything we say — you'll offend her.'

They drank their orange juice and had just finished the cereal when the old lady appeared again bringing a succulent cooked breakfast which she set before them.

'Now I don't want you to think that I know everything you say — or that I'm a witch or anything like that' she said cheerfully. 'There's no mystery about how I knew your names and no magic either. Just telescopes, carrier pigeons and putting two and two

together.' She smiled at them and they were speechless with astonishment.

'My son is captain down on the boat you saw in the bay. He has a strong telescope and doesn't miss much. We've carrier pigeons on board and we've also friends in Heartsease who send us messages — sometimes by pigeon and sometimes through the tradespeople. Fowler has reward notices about Driftwood pasted up all over town and Herbert, and Hazy came over by ferry first thing this morning. They were making a dreadful fuss about Sorrel who had run away with this boy who had threatened them with a poker and locked them in a bedroom.

We knew that when you arrived you would be tired. You would have come ashore at the dunes and slept for a bit then. So my son had his telescope trained on the cliff path looking for you. Simple you see — no mystery at all.'

'But I said you might be a witch' gasped Sorrel.

'Did you my dear? I'm not the least bit surprised. You'd be bound to be uneasy — and children always think about gingerbread houses and witches and things. It's all those fairy stories they teach you. Well, I'm not a witch. In fact I don't approve of witches at all. My name is Melody. My husband died many years ago and I live with my sister, Harmony. Our home is called Dove Cottage. We always say that our father has a lot to answer for — such silly names! Now enjoy your breakfast. Do you eat toast? Good. The marmalade is homemade."

CHAPTER 9
GLUMMIT

G lummit was a sly man, cunning and devious, quick witted in an emergency. Fowler had described him as a 'pitiful wreck of a man'. Certainly he had a large paunch and a small head — so you could say he was egg shaped. But under his sandy hair and behind his shifty eyes lay an artful brain.

When Driftwood had scattered the contents of his till, Glummit had been furious, but greedy though he was, self preservation came first. So while the search was on for Driftwood, Glummit was hidden high up in his own haystack, well away from trouble. While he lay in hiding he did a lot of thinking.

The result of his thinking was that not long after Strug and Stumble set out for Diamede, Glummit also took the road. He was riding an old farmhorse, a safe mount which would not shy, or gallop off, but which plodded on its way, head hanging down, as though life were totally uninteresting. Glummit was not bound for

91

Diamede, but for Heartsease. His destination was Threld Manor, Fowler's headquarters within the cluster of buildings that Sorrel referred to as 'Potlot.'

Threld Manor, an extensive property overlooking Heartsease Bay, had been the country residence of the Threld family for generations. The King and Queen delighted to holiday there, but since Fowler's rise to power, nothing had been seen of either of them. The Manor had been built centuries ago in the grounds of a still more ancient castle. Only the keep of the castle, remained, but since Fowler's arrival, this had been restored and refurbished. Behind the Manor were other buildings, all interconnected — some above ground, others with passages below ground. There was also a tunnel in the mountainside leading to the quartz mines which were the source of Fowler's prosperity.

Glummit had plenty of time to take in the splendour of the ancient red brick Manor with its oriel windows, and ornamented chimneys. Once his horse had plodded up the steep hill, it was quite out of breath And when it reached the long drive within the ornate iron gates, it almost refused to go any further.

Threld Manor was a splendid sight. Fowler had lavished care upon his headquarters. High from the grey granite keep, hung a great colourful flag, with his name blazoned in letters so large that they were clearly visible from the town. There was a stiff breeze that day and Glummit could easily read the huge words, 'Fowler's Pharmaceuticals.'

Glummit chewed nervously on his sandy moustache, but persisted on his way towards the great main doorway. Leaving the horse tethered to a convenient post, he climbed the great staircase and tugged at the bell pull. A butler in full attire opened the door and gazed down at Glummit with a dispassionate stare.

'Tradespeople use the back entrance' he declared, and began to close the door again.

Glummit was unabashed. 'Don't give me none of your lip' he retorted. 'You're only a Dreird. You're to give this message to Fowler. Tell 'im. I know what 'e wants and I know 'ow to get it!'

'Wait there' said the butler majestically and closed the door.

Glummit waited, glancing about him with shifty eyes, yet stubbornly standing his ground and refusing to be intimidated. He was confident that if only he could keep his wits about him Fowler would listen. This proved to be true, for within a short while Glummit was ushered into Threld Manor, and passed from one department to another until he found himself in a room high up in the castle keep. Here Fowler confronted him.

'Two matters' said Fowler 'First you will tell me all you know, second you shall drink the pledge of loyalty. The second shall be first. Drink, then speak. So shall I hear the truth from you.'

Glummit waved Slobbit away. His voice was servile, but confident.

'I ain't drinking nothing. Begging your pardon Mr Fowler Sir, but it wouldn't be to your advantage for me to drink it. You see Mr Fowler Sir, I've sussed out one of your little secrets like.'

Fowler eyed him coldly. But Glummit saw that he was at least listening.

'These 'ere Dreirds' said Glummit 'You've got a problem with them ain't you. That's why you get on better with Slobbit.'

He glanced furtively at Fowler, but then fixed his gaze on the fireplace to Fowler's left. He was feeling very frightened, but was determined not to show it.

'The trouble with Dreirds' he declared 'is that they ain't got no feelings. They does what you want, but they don't care any more. They ain't interested in anything. Just like my old 'orse. Only Black Tor scared 'em, and that's got you puzzling I guess. But what I want to say Mr Fowler Sir,' and now the words came in a rush, 'what I want to say is 'ow you need me. A man who cares for your interests like.'

He shot another glance at Fowler's inscrutable face and played his trump card.

'What if I get Driftwood for you — the Dreirds don't know what 'e looks like. I do. The Dreirds don't care if they catch 'im or not, but it matters to me. I want to get my hands on that kid for what 'appened at the Tipsy Goose. And I don't want the £5 reward — though I wouldn't say no to it. I want to work for you, Mr Fowler Sir, that's what I want. Full time job. No being turned into a Dreird. 'Ow about it Sir, what do you think? It's a fair offer ain't it?'

There was a long pause, then Fowler spoke.

'Attempt to trick me and you will be silenced for ever. Serve me well, and I will show you favour. Bring Driftwood to me!'

Fowler swept from the room. The interview was over. Slobbit removed wet fingers from his mouth in order to speak.

'Slobbit tell Dreirds. Do what you want. You — me work together.'

He leered at Glummit, their faces so close that the stench of Slobbit's breath engulfed Glummit and he struggled not to pull a face at its foul smell.

'O.K. partner. Let's get on with it.' They left the room together.

The two of them cordially hated each other from the very beginning. Glummit loathed everything about Slobbit — the beastly way he messed about in his mouth with his fingers, his dreadful breath and unpleasant scratching habits. Glummit was never quite sure whether Slobbit was animal or man and he feared his strength.

Slobbit deeply resented Glummit. He understood dimly that the man's brain was far more devious and subtle than his own and felt endangered by Glummit's cunning. He could smell Glummit, and Glummit didn't only smell of beer and farms and horses. He smelt of treachery and greed and dark twisted ambition. If Fowler decided to favour Glummit above the noble Slobbit, the loyal Slobbit — then so much the worse for Fowler.

But there was work to be done, a quarry to be hunted. For the present the two partners' interests coincided. Glummit had characteristically kept something secret. He now decided it was safe to take Slobbit into his confidence.

One of Driftwood's delights at the Tipsy Goose had been to play darts. He was very good, having a steady hand and a clear eye. Well he had been playing earlier on the fateful evening when the press gang came and had been using a cloth to rub out the scores on the blackboard. Nobody else had used the cloth all evening. Slobbit snuffled at the rag Glummit offered him, then, when the chalk dust shot up his nose, he let out an immense sneeze. Glummit, staggered back wiping his face with his arm.

'Slobbit smell him good. Slobbit find him now!'

The partnership was underway. The ill assorted pair set off, mounted on fresh horses, and accompanied by a dozen strong Dreirds. Glummit reasoned that Driftwood would have avoided the town so they began checking the paths that led up into the hills. At the beach, Slobbit dismounted again and again to snuffle at the ground.

Soon they came across the dinghy carefully concealed in the bushes. Glummit was impatient with the time that Slobbit spent snuffling around the boat. But Slobbit was the expert here. He sniffed the mainsheet that Sorrel had held and the jib sheets that Driftwood had held. His acute sense of smell told him many things.

He detected the faint odour of Chuckle who had built the boat and could smell coal dust from the fire. He also picked up the delicious scents of the succulent meal at Dunroamin — not least of all, the subtle and most delectable perfume of the apple pie. The tiniest crumbs of pastry had stuck to Driftwood and then fallen into the boat. But they brought to Slobbit visions of glorious food, the like of which he had never tasted. Saliva dripped from his mouth into the sand dunes. A new ambition had entered his life. To track down the maker of that apple pie.

Once Slobbit had the scent, it did not take long to track the pair down. Once they'd located Dove Cottage, they left Dreirds hiding among the trees to keep watch, and returned to Threld Manor to consult with Fowler for further orders. Had this been a remote country district like Black Tor, they would not have hesitated to raid the Cottage and burn it to the ground — although they would probably have waited till nightfall.

But at Heartsease, it was not Fowler's policy to intimidate and tyrannise. Certainly, Dreirds maintained firm order and criminals were summarily punished — individuals might be threatened and the occasional person disappear. But Fowler preferred to be regarded as the benefactor of Heartsease — respected by the Town Councillors, presenting prizes to school children. His own prosperity was linked with the prosperity of the town, so he posed as an honourable citizen. Fowler was pleased with Glummit's plan, and it was agreed that the cottage would be kept under surveillance until the following morning.

'*I* wonder if you could make an apple pie for us, Sorrel' suggested Melody. 'I've got a few people coming round this evening and I'd love to give them a slice of pie before they go.'

'I'll make the pastry this morning and cook it last thing tonight so it's fresh' replied Sorrel.

'That will be lovely, dear. My son and a few others are coming from the ship. We meet and sing a few songs about the Daylord and talk about the old stories. Would you like to join us?'

Sorrel shook her head.

'No thank you. I'll have to concentrate on the apple pie.'

Just as it was beginning to get dark there was a knock on the door and the sound of laughing voices. It was the Captain and some of the crew from the ship. They crowded into the room, talking and joking. Sorrel stayed in the kitchen. She decided she would meet

them later when their meeting was over. After a while
the hubbub quietened down and the meeting began.
Now and again Sorrel heard them singing.

She recognised one or two tunes from her days at
primary school but thought it was all a bit quaint.
They weren't anything like the Dice playing crowd she
had known at Heartsease. Still, if Driftwood wanted to
get mixed up with them, that was his business. No
doubt they were harmless enough. She put on an
apron, preheated the oven and put the finishing touches
to her apple pie.

Driftwood decided to go to the meeting and took to
Melody's son straight away. He had curly black hair
and the weather-beaten face and tanned complexion
of a seafaring man. His friends were good humoured
friendly people. The talk about the Daylord interested
him. He didn't understand everything, but was eager
to learn. And he could piece bits together because of
his conversation with Chuckle.

When the meeting ended Sorrel came in with the
apple pie and Harmony followed with coffee and tea.
The apple pie was a great success. Hazy Humple had
never said a word about Sorrel's superb cooking and
Sorrel felt a little embarrassed at the praise she
received. On the other hand, she knew that not many
cooks could beat her when it came to pastry making.

She was humming cheerfully to herself as she
returned to the kitchen to get a tray to collect the
empties. As she stood in the kitchen she happened to
glance towards the window that overlooked the garden. A monstrous face was pushed against the window

pane from the outside. It had slobbering wet lips, and wildly staring eyes. She had never seen such an apparition. Her blood ran cold and she screamed. People came rushing into the kitchen.

'What is it?' said Melody hugging Sorrel. 'It was horrible!' sobbed Sorrel, burying her face in Melody's shoulder. 'I saw two great goggling eyes. One bigger than the other and a horrible snout pushed hard against the window pane. Spit was trickling down the glass!'

'Slobbit!' exclaimed Driftwood.

'You never said he looked like that!' cried Sorrel.

'Well I suppose if he pushed his nose against the window he'd look worse than usual' said Driftwood 'No one could call him good looking at the best of times.'

Melody's son, snatched a torch and rushed out into the garden. Some of the other men went with him. They hunted up and down and searched around. But there was no trace of Slobbit at all.

'Never fear' said the Captain. 'One or two of us will stay here tonight.'

But Melody would have none of that.

'Nonsense' she said. 'Your place is with the boat. Those shields may arrive any day. You know that. You must be ready and so must the crew. We're quite safe. The Daylord will shelter us.'

'Oh please let the Captain stay!' pleaded Sorrel. 'I'm really frightened now and I'd feel better if he were here.'

Melody was surprisingly firm.

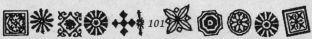

'I'm sorry my dear, but you must believe that you're safe here. Big issues are involved. Things you don't yet understand. In any case, there isn't the slightest reason to be frightened. You see we're protected by the birds.'

That was just too much! Sorrel had known all along that these people were a bit weird — with all their talks about the Daylord. Now they were going to trust their safety to a few carrier pigeons! She'd had a hard day and Slobbit had given her a real fright. Something inside her snapped and her eyes blazed furiously.

'You're dead right!' she exclaimed, choking back tears of anger. 'I don't understand. I don't understand at all.' She rushed from the room and slammed her bedroom door.

'Shall I go up to her?' asked Harmony. 'No' replied Melody. 'She's just overtired. It's all been too much. Leave her. She'll be better in the morning.' But, for once, she was wrong.

Later Driftwood lingered behind to talk to Melody when everyone else had gone. The room seemed comfortable, and the lamps were cosy. Melody had taken out her knitting and seemed very relaxed.

'What did you mean about the birds?' Driftwood wanted to know.

Melody knitted a few stitches before replying — as if she was making up her mind about something. Then she answered,

'Some of them are just carrier pigeons, but not all. Some are the Daylord's doves.'

'I don't see how doves can protect you' said Driftwood.

'They're such peaceful birds, aren't they?' Melody agreed. 'But these are special and they have a wonderful way of spreading their wings. There's nothing to be anxious about, Driftwood. This cottage is protected by birds flying.'

Driftwood felt more mystified than ever, but he could see that Melody wasn't going to say any more about the birds, so he changed the subject. The talk in the meeting had set him thinking about Black Tor, so he asked whether she could explain why he had never felt the terror until the night that Fowler came.

'It troubled me again this morning — when I had that nap on the beach. I fell asleep thinking that I really shouldn't have threatened the Humples with that poker and I felt rotten about it. Then while I was asleep I dreamt that a great piece of paper was blowing across my face. It had all sorts of bad things about me written on it. I couldn't read half of them, but somehow I knew that they were all true.'

Melody put down her knitting and gazed at him over the top of her spectacles.

'What you need,' she said gently 'is to see the Daylord's pearl.'

'Do you mean this?' asked Driftwood, who fished out the pouch and produced the pearl. He looked at it in amazement. It was definitely larger than it had been, although it was still much smaller than a pea. But his surprise was nothing compared with Melody's. She was so astonished that her glasses almost fell off her nose.

'Wherever did you get that?' she demanded.

Driftwood told her the whole story and she listened fascinated.

'When we talk about "seeing the pearl"' she said, 'we really mean that we know and understand. I never thought that I'd actually see it for myself.'

'Do you want to hold it?' asked Driftwood.

She shook her head. 'It isn't right for me to touch it.' she replied. 'You must hold fast till ...' she broke off. 'Oh, but I am so thrilled to have had a glimpse of it. Now listen to me Driftwood. The Black Tor isn't evil. It's good, but it can't bring comfort. It's the pearl that brings peace — not because of what it is, but because of what the Daylord did in another place and another time. Hold that pearl fast and the Black Tor won't trouble you. For its power meets that of the pearl and is satisfied.'

'But the pearl seems to have got bigger since I first looked at it.' said Driftwood.

Melody smiled. 'The Daylord's things do have a way of growing — pearls, birds, horses, all sorts of things grow as he wants them to. Not everybody notices that they're growing. Some just can't see it at all. The only thing that some people notice is the withering and the dying. But the Daylord makes things that grow.'

'Strug and Stumble make coffins and funeral monuments' said Driftwood.

'That's because they lived so long at Black Tor.' replied Melody. 'They would have done much better to join us down here at Dove Cottage.'

Driftwood nodded thoughtfully. 'Come to think of it,' he said, 'they seemed to make a lot more coffins than they really needed — just as though they felt miserable somehow.'

'Black Tor does that' said Melody. 'It belongs to the Daylord and it's good — but not a place I would like to live — at any rate, not yet!'

After Driftwood had gone to bed Melody went out into the quiet garden and stood for a while watching the great white birds soaring far overhead. Peace settled upon her heart like the down of soft feathers.

The next morning everything seemed happy again. Driftwood came down to find Melody in the kitchen. Outside the window a man was busy with a wash leather. He was tall and had silver grey hair, a beak of a nose, a sallow complexion and a gentle smile. He wore a blue baize apron and was polishing away at the glass.

'That's our window cleaner' said Melody. 'The Daylord must have sent him over this morning. He heard that Slobbit had been dribbling on our window and has come to make everything clean and sparkling again.'

Driftwood's mind was on breakfast and he took no more notice of the stranger outside. He started to cut bread for the toast and was busy when Harmony came into the room holding a letter.

'Whatever's the matter Harmony?' asked Melody.

'It's addressed to Driftwood' said Harmony. 'Sorrel has gone and this was lying on her pillow.'

Driftwood opened the envelope.

'Dear Driftwood' the letter ran. 'I have decided to run away. I'm so grateful to everyone — you've all

been very kind. But I know that I don't belong. I've had a terrible night — so frightened that Slobbit might come back. I can't trust the Daylord like Mrs Melody. I know that you belong with the boat people, but I don't. I'm no good to anyone, so I'm getting out of your lives. Thank you for a glimpse into your lovely world, but its not for me! Goodbye. Sorrel. P.S. I was wrong to call you "brother". We've nothing in common.'

'I must go after her straight away' cried Driftwood. 'She can't have gone far. She wouldn't have left in the dark.'

'No, Driftwood' said Mrs Melody sadly. 'You must let her run now. Her story is only just beginning. You have the pearl, and your first duty is to get it to Diamede.'

Harmony was looking out of the window. 'Calm has finished the windows' she said as if nothing had happened.

'Who did you say?' cried Driftwood.

'Calm' replied Harmony.

'But I want to speak to him!' cried Driftwood. 'I think he may be able to help us.'

'He left when I came in with the letter' said Harmony. 'I think he may be helping already.'

Dry eyed. Hard faced and determined, Sorrel was hurrying along the road to the village of Grimwald. It was many miles from Heartsease and it would take all day to get there. But at least she had cut all ties and was free.

'You're really on your own now, Sorrel my girl' she told herself soberly.

In this she was wrong, for at a safe distance far behind, an old carpenter, with silver hair and a blue apron was leading along a fine horse, a horse that seemed far too splendid for such a simple tradesman. It nuzzled Calm's arm as he walked, and he spoke to it.

'Patience Spindrift, remember we can't interfere till the Daylord says "NOW."' The horse responded with a gentle whinny as if it understood every word.

CHAPTER 11
SNARED!

❀

The Dreirds had permitted Sorrel to leave the cottage. She was of little interest to them. Calm they had not seen at all, because he was no ordinary carpenter and travelled by another road and another way.

However when the milkman arrived at the corner of the lane that led to Dove Cottage, he found a group of workmen and a barrier blockading the road. Glummit, at his most apologetic, offered to deliver the bottles himself. He explained that he was the foreman, and needed to visit the cottage in any case. Suspecting nothing, the milkman went on his way, glad to have saved a little time. As soon as he had gone, the Dreirds began to remove the barrier.

Glummit intended to introduce himself as the new milkman and to bluff his way into the cottage to meet Driftwood. However, he was saved any difficulty by the fact that Driftwood himself answered the door.

'Glummit' he exclaimed, recognising the landlord at once. 'Why are you here? What's happened about the Tipsy Goose?'

'Fancy meeting you!' exclaimed Glummit. 'It's a small world ain't it. I've turned milkman as you can see. It's terrible at 'ome at present — nothing but Dreirds everywhere. I've put up the shutters at the Tipsy Goose and done a bunk. "Get out while you can" I says to myself. "There'll be nothing but trouble if you stay on 'ere." So I saddled my old 'orse and came over to 'eartsease to get myself a job.' His shifty eyes fixed on Driftwood for a moment and then transferred their attention to a nearby rose bush.

'Wot a surprise meeting you though! Of all the the 'ouses on me milk round, almost the first door I knock on, there's you inside. Whoever would have thought it?'

He sucked his sandy moustache and rambled on. 'Terrible news about Strug and Stumble though ain't it.'

'What news!' exclaimed Driftwood.

'Ain't you 'eard? Fowlers got 'em in chains in Threld Manor. That's what my friend up at the Manor said when I delivered the milk there early this morning. Won't give 'em any food neither. Says they've got to tell 'im the secret of Black Tor. Crying shame ain't it? Two nice respectable gents. Not my sort, of course. They'd never come near the Tipsy Goose. All the same, I don't bear them any ill will. Any'ow, take care Driftwood, I've got work to do.'

With those words, Glummit picked up the empty bottles and turned to go.

'Hey, wait Glummit' begged Driftwood. 'This is dreadful, I've got to do something to rescue them.'

Glummit seemed to hesitate. He glanced shiftily about him, then lowered his voice.

'I'd like to 'elp you if I could Driftwood. I'd be sorry to think of those two poor old gents dying in the dungeon — not when they've been so kind to you since you were a nipper and all. Tell you what. If you was to come straight away, and not say a word to the folks 'ere, I think I could find a way to get you into Threld Manor and get you into that dungeon too. There's a wench there, it was 'er was telling me about the old gentlemen. She owes me a favour from the old days and I reckon we could smuggle you in between us. You'd 'ave to promise not to give us away whatever 'appened. That's why you mustn't say anything to the folks 'ere. You'd put them in danger and me and my gal in danger as well. You just give 'em the milk and tell 'em you'll be back in a minute. Meet me down the end of the lane.'

Before Driftwood had time to answer or argue, Glummit had turned on his heel and was gone.

'Swallowed it like a child, Slobbit! He'll be down 'ere in a minute, you mark my words. Right taken in 'e was. When it comes to spinning a yarn, Glummit's your man. Tell those Dreirds to be ready to grab 'im.' Glummit rubbed his hands with glee.

Sure enough, before many minutes had passed, Driftwood came through the garden gate and began to hurry down the lane. The Dreirds who had been hiding in the woods, surrounded him and in no time he was

gagged, trussed hand and foot and bundled over the saddle of a horse.

Driftwood had plenty of time to ask himself why he had been foolish enough to believe Glummit's tale. He'd been taken in because he believed Glummit was a friend, or if not a friend at least someone who had no reason to harm him or wish him ill. But as he struggled with the cruel ropes that bit into his wrists, he realised that he was worth £5 to Glummit. Indeed, his successful capture might be the beginning of a new career for Glummit in the service of Fowler. He had been duped, and betrayed. His only comfort was gleaned from a conversation between Glummit and Slobbit — his guardians were not under arrest at all. At least Strug and Stumble were still free, even if Driftwood was due for an uncomfortable meeting with Fowler.

Glummit was not allowed to be in attendance when Fowler met Driftwood. Fowler who was himself expert in treachery placed little trust in Glummit's loyalty — although he was prepared to reward him, since the man's cunning would be useful to him. So apart from Slobbit, no one was allowed to enter the suite of rooms in the tower where Fowler lived in luxury. These rooms were constructed within the battlements at the very top of the keep. They had a commanding view of the town of Heartsease and the blue waters of the bay.

Driftwood was released from his bonds and admitted to the inner sanctum where he was given some minutes to await Fowler's arrival.

In front of the window was a splendid desk of green quartz. There were bookcases against the walls and tasteful pictures in gilded frames. The pale green ceiling rose to a central apex where a strong hook had been screwed into the roof timbers. In an alcove, lit by carefully arranged concealed lighting, stood a life size doll. She was wearing a ball gown and jewels glinted at her neck. One hand held a wine glass to her lips and her sparkling eyes glanced out merrily above the rim. She seemed to be in the very act of drinking someone's good health. The other arm hung loosely at her side and in its gentle clasp, a delicate red rosebud protruded from finely manicured fingers. Her feet were in dainty high heeled shoes. Even her eyelashes were perfectly modelled and the hair curled gently over her shoulder.

Driftwood had never seen a statue like this before. The life like effect of the image startled him considerably. It almost seemed that the eyes were alive. There was also something about this beautiful woman that stirred a memory in him, but he couldn't quite be sure what it was.

On one of the bookcases was a large bowl of fruit. The smell was pleasant and Driftwood remembered that it was getting near lunch time. However he had no intention of eating or drinking anything in Fowler's apartment.

He walked towards the great desk. Several items lay on it. A heavy quartz inkstand, a large blotting pad, a desk lamp and a paper knife in a quartz tray. The handle of the knife was of reddish quartz and the blade was made of finely sharpened steel. Its point was as sharp as a needle. Behind the desk was a

comfortably padded black leather swivel chair. Open on the desk was a catalogue advertising the wares of 'Fowlers Pharmaceuticals.'

Driftwood began to skim through the book as quickly as he could. If he could understand Fowler's business interests, maybe he would find a way to outwit the villain. He soon realised that Fowler had established a very extensive and flourishing organisation. He was trading with the world beyond the islands. There was a chemical division dealing mainly in ointments, sun lotions and beauty preparations. Then there was the quartz exporting section — page after page of pictures of ornamental objects made from quartz.

There was an architectural section too. This described the design of different quartz houses. It seemed here that trade was strictly limited to the locality of Heartsease. Some of the houses could be built cheaply enough for modest incomes, others were wildly extravagant. The difference depended mainly on the transparency of the quartz used. Dark coloured, semi opaque quartz was fairly cheap, but clear crystal quartz was exorbitantly expensive. To his astonishment, Driftwood realised that the most rich, famous, and important people of Heartsease would be living in houses where almost everything they did would be clearly visible to the public.

The final section listed goods which were not directly manufactured by Fowler Pharmaceuticals. This was the trading division. The catalogue of merchandise seemed endless — gold, silver, precious stones, pearls, fine linens, citron wood, articles of ivory, even exotic animals like monkeys and peacocks — the list went on and on.

Apart from the houses of Heartsease, the brochure seemed entirely devoted to luxury goods. Fowler's Pharmaceuticals did not deal in genuine medicines, nor food, nor ordinary clothes, nor useful machinery.

'It's a load of junk!' Driftwood muttered to himself scornfully.

Fowler entered the room so quietly that Driftwood was taken by surprise. Fowler had changed his clothes completely and now wore a business man's suit with a neat pin stripe. This was the first time that Driftwood had ever had a clear sight of his face. It was pale and thin, with a beak-like nose and a cruel mouth. His complexion beneath the skin was slightly lemon coloured, but his eyes were alive with intelligence. His forehead was high, his hair thin and swept back at the temples but long at the neck. It was his hands with those lean sensitive fingers that held Driftwood's attention. Each knuckle had a lump on it. There appeared to be some nodule or growth beneath the skin.

'You have been a tiresome nuisance Driftwood' Fowler began dispassionately. 'However, you have also shown considerable initiative. I have a position for a young man like yourself provided you are willing to be trained. I need someone who will put Fowler Pharmaceuticals before his personal interests and who will give total loyalty to the firm. I'm going to make you an offer. Listen carefully, because if you refuse it, you will not leave this room alive.'

Driftwood swallowed. 'If I could make a suggestion Sir,' he replied politely. 'I would much rather not hear the offer. Then I could go quietly back to Black Tor and mind my own business.'

Fowler laughed drily.

'No doubt you would prefer that. But I have always followed a sound principle. I take no foolish risks. You represent what I call a "loose end." I never leave those lying around. Your life is not worth more than £5 to me. That is the reward I offered. You are of trivial importance, but I could train you to be a useful executive and as such you would be rewarded. So we are faced with two matters, and the second shall be first.'

Fowler paced the room, and gestured with a sweep of his arm towards the window.

'There is a great world out there, Driftwood. Beyond this small group of islands which we call the Strangelands, there are other lands and other islands. My purpose is to trade and I need a young representative to travel for me. The Dreirds are obedient but dull. They show no initiative. I could use an intelligent young operative like you so I'm offering you a share in my great secret.'

Fowler seated himself comfortably in the chair behind the desk and went on.

'Some years ago when I was a young nobleman at the court of King Threld, I explored deep into the caverns below Diamede. I had no companion but my mastiff. In the cavern I made a discovery. Over long ages of time, a pool of Dreadwater has appeared deep in a crater below this cavern. It has formed from liquid which slowly steeps through the ancient rocks, making stalactites and stalagmites. Should one drip fall upon anything, that object turns to quartz. Glass is the only exception that I've found.

Immediately I perceived the possibilities for great power. I told no one of my discovery. Instead I began a careful series of experiments. You will appreciate that there were great risks to myself. One contact with the Dreadwater would have destroyed me.' Here Fowler shuddered.

'My first aim was to find the secret of immunity — and I am still seeking this. However I have found the next best thing. I have discovered a barrier cream which apply to my skin each day. It has certain drawbacks — as you will see from the condition of my hands. Nevertheless it protects me from the danger of accidental splashes. I can handle Dreadwater with safety, although to drink it or be immersed in it for a long period would be another matter. The principle of the cream is simple enough. Basically it is quartz itself, finely powdered till it acts like a pigment in paint. Only the best translucent quartz is effective, so the cream is too valuable to be used indiscriminately. Of course, the other constituents are totally secret, known only to myself.

Protected by the cream, I was able to proceed to further experiments. I found that by precise dilution it was possible to achieve a dosage which was no longer fatal, but turned only certain brain cells to quartz. The result was a pleasingly docile and obedi-

ent servant creature whom I call a Dreird. This was progress, but I still needed the elixir which would guarantee my own personal safety.'

Fowler rose from his chair and began restlessly pacing the room.

'I sought that antidote with the same desperation as the early Alchemists sought to find the secret which would turn all things to gold. Working alone and under great difficulties, I achieved some remarkable successes with the Dreadwater — in particular the hunting cats. Slobbit is also the result of one of my experiments — a highly successful operation as far as he is concerned, although he isn't as intellectually bright as I could wish. But although I discovered other secrets, the remedy for the Dreadwater still eludes me."

'What made you suppose that there was an antidote to the Dreadwater?' asked Driftwood.

Fowler paced the room again and stood looking out into the bay, his back turned towards Driftwood.

'Nothing but a legend' he replied. 'There's an ancient myth about a being from another place and another time. Someone called the Daylord who obtained a mysterious remedy by a dangerous journey. Of course men of science like myself despise the superstitious nonsense which simple minds believe. Yet ...' he paused 'if it were possible to get at the truth that lies behind the myth, it may well refer to the antidote. The legend says nothing of the Dreadwater of course, but there is a vague reference to wrong being righted at Diamede.' He shrugged. 'At any rate the story encourages me to persevere in my experiments because if there is an antidote, its secret must belong to me alone.'

Fowler swung round to face Driftwood. 'So as I said we are faced with two matters. The second was the secret of Dreadwater. The first is your moment of choice. What do you say? If you become my agent travelling abroad, I can promise you great power and wealth. Refuse that offer and I shall use the Dreadwater to turn you to quartz.'

Driftwood knew that he would never become Fowler's agent, but he was not eager to sign his own death warrant.

'Give me more time' he pleaded. 'I need to think this through.'

Fowler smiled pleasantly.

'By all means.' He went to the door and Slobbit came into the room.

'String him up!' Fowler ordered. There was a brief struggle but Driftwood was no match for Slobbit. Before he knew what was happening, he found himself hanging upside down from a pulley in the ceiling. A rope like a hangman's noose was round his ankle. It passed through the pulley and down to a cleat at the far side of the room. Beneath his head Slobbit placed a basin made of green quartz. Taking the stopper from a jar made of the same material, he carefully poured a quantity of liquid into the bowl.

'Dreadwater' said Fowler. 'In its concentrated form it is more dangerous than the most corrosive acid. I have always understood that a generous supply of

blood to the brain is a help to clear thinking. You are now in a position to think very clearly. It's lunchtime now. During the afternoon Slobbit will return periodically to lower you a little nearer to the Dreadwater. This will aid your concentration. The offer is still there. Give me your promise that you will work for me and I will release you.'

Fowler and Slobbit left the room. Driftwood was caught like a rabbit in a snare, hung by one leg from the rope. As he slowly revolved first one way and then the other, he frantically tried to think of a way to escape.

CHAPTER 12
GRIMWALD

*I*t was early afternoon by the time Sorrel reached Grimwald. The village was laid out something like the spokes of a cartwheel. Lanes leading from surrounding villages converged on the central square. The houses — most of which were centuries old — had been built higgledy piggledy, with no attempt at planning. It was a big sleepy overgrown village, very different from the brilliance of Heartsease.

In the market square stood an open building with a roof supported on aged timbers. It was presumably some kind of corn exchange. A public house fronted one side of the square which was entirely paved with cobble stones. There was a horse trough with an old iron pump, the handle painted black, but rusting. Just beyond the corn exchange was a wall and close to it an old set of stocks where delinquents of the past used to be imprisoned, their legs pinioned, to receive whatever punishment the populace chose to heap on them.

Perhaps in reference to this, the public house was called 'The Pillory' — a pleasant enough building, ancient and ivy covered. It had wooden benches outside and leaded lights. The signboard showed the picture of some hapless yokel, his head and hands trapped in the pillory.

Sorrel looked above the door and noted the landlord's name. In weatherworn gold leaf were the words 'Harry Sleazle, licensed to purvey wines and spirits.' She tried the door. It swung open.

'Mr Sleazle?' Sorrel asked.

Harry Sleazle stood broom in hand, his shirtsleeves rolled up to reveal muscular tattooed arms. He was a huge man — broad as well as tall, red headed with a vigorous beard of the same colour.

'We're closed' he grunted, his voice deep and throaty.

'I was wondering ...' said Sorrel timidly, 'whether you've got any work.'

The landlord eyed her curiously and rubbed a bleary eye with his shirtsleeve.

'Lot of use a li'll shrimp like yer 'ud be' he replied scornfully.

Colour rose in Sorrel's cheeks and her chin came up. 'I'm stronger than I look' she said defiantly. 'I know how to work.'

The landlord continued to stare at her. 'Tell yer wot. I'll give yer a try. No pay mind —times is 'ard. But there's allus a bite to eat in the kitchen, bangers, that sort o' thing. Keep your 'ands off the steak, that's for the customers — the gentry like. But yer won' t go

'ungry, and there's a bed yer can 'ave up in the loft.
The customers is a rough lot, most of 'em, but generous when they've 'ad a few, which is most nights!
You'll pick up something off 'em by way o' pocket
money.'

'Thanks' said Sorrel briefly. She was famished and
decided that if she didn't like the place she needn't
stay more than a day or two. Harry Sleazle didn't
improve on acquaintance. He was a loud bullying sort
of man., his eyes bloodshot with sampling his own
goods.

Sorrel found plenty of mess in the kitchen and a
great deal of washing and tidying up to do. At least
Hazy Humple had been tidy, scrupulously clean and
neat. Sorrel found her own lips pursing with disapproval — just as Hazy's would have done. She guessed
that at night the kitchen would be running with cock-
roaches.

Finding her way into the larder, she managed to get
something to eat. She didn't cook anything but gnawed
away at a hunk of bread and dripping as she hurried
about cleaning and tidying. She knew she must make
a good first impression if she was to be allowed to stay.
It would be opening time soon and the first customers
would be arriving.

Driftwood felt cramped and in agony. Slobbit had
already returned once to lower him a fraction towards
the great container of concentrated Dreadwater. To
begin with he had let the rope go with a rush and
Driftwood had thought that he would be plunged into
the liquid. But at the last moment, with a jeer of

laughter Slobbit checked the rope and pulled him up almost as high as ever. The jerk had tightened the noose even more.

When Slobbit had gone, Driftwood had an idea. Reaching up to his free leg, he managed to remove his shoe. Holding it by the tip, he tried to reach the water. It was too far below. He unthreaded the shoe lace, and tied it through the two eyeholes nearest to the tip of the shoe. Then he dangled it down, gripping the end of the lace very tightly with the end wound round his finger.

Cautiously he dangled it closer and closer to the Dreadwater. What would happen? he wondered. He would have to risk everything. The heel of the shoe dipped gently into the Dreadwater. Fowler had not been bluffing. In an instant the whole shoe turned into quartz. But it was still the same shape. To his relief the shoe lace, which had not been in contact with the liquid, remained unaffected. He allowed the shoe to dip further into the Dreadwater and then raised it carefully. The quartz shoe now had Dreadwater in it. He must be very careful indeed. There was no danger in touching the dry end of the shoe, but if even one dribble of Dreadwater were to run from the shoe and touch his flesh, it would be the end of him.

It was like handling highly corrosive acid. Gritting his teeth with pain and taking infinite care he began to swing himself at the end of the rope, like the pendulum in Glummit's clock at the Tipsy Goose. He was aiming to reach a point where he could suddenly reach up and empty the contents of the shoe over the rope which led downwards from the pulley and away to the door. It took several swings, but with a flick of the wrist he managed to soak a portion of the rope with liquid. For fear of being splashed, he dropped the shoe immediately.

He was almost too successful. The portion of rope that had turned to brown quartz was alien to the dry rope and immediately began to tear away strand by strand. Driftwood only just had time to swing clear of the bowl before he fell in a crumpled heap onto the floor. Fortunately he didn't break any bones.

He took the paper knife from the desk. Picking up the black chair, he used it to smash through the window. Then he got out onto the roof of the keep. Hurriedly he pulled at the ropes on the tall flagpole and lowered the flag. He guessed that he had about fifteen minutes before Slobbit returned to the room. There was ample material in the flag, but would his idea work? Slashing with the paper knife and tying knots between the rope and the silken material of the flag, he began to construct a makeshift parachute. He knotted a 'Bosun's chair' to support his legs and then worked his way up onto the parapet.

He was at a dizzy height but felt confident that the parachute would break his fall to some degree. Whether it would work properly could only be proved by jumping. He knew that if he delayed, he would lose his courage.

'One two three, here we go!' he cried and leaped from the parapet.

Seated in a sheltered spot on an adjacent roof two workmen were enjoying their lunch. Sheltering be-

hind one of the large chimneys they were invisible from the ground but had an excellent view of Driftwood's escape.

'Whatever will that boy think of next!' exclaimed Chuckle with amazement.

'He'll fall and break his neck for sure!' cried Calm.

But Chuckle already had his spirit level in his hands and he raised it and held it parallel to the ground. The makeshift parachute suddenly flapped and opened gracefully as though invisible strings connected it to the bar in Chuckle's hands.

'Up a bit, gently does it' murmured Chuckle. He tilted the spirit level a fraction and the parachute drifted higher as if in response.

'Aye, up in the air we go, young Sir. Happen as how you need to have good friends a-looking after you. You would have killed yourself otherwise, I wouldn't wonder. Now Calm, my old friend, where do we send him next?' Calm, more relaxed now, was pouring tea from a flask.

'The Daylord needs him in Grimwald by early evening' he replied.

Chuckle swung the spirit level and the parachute circled like a bird high in the air.

'Grimwald it is then — and he must have time to buy himself some shoes when he first gets there. So we'll let him drift down gently right near the outskirts of town. Off you go young Sir.' He watched as Driftwood floated off like thistledown. The carpenter chuckled.

'He'll have a job explaining as how he came to lose that there shoe!'

❀

CHAPTER 13
HARRY SLEAZLE

❀

*B*ecause of weakness, Strug and Stumble travelled slowly. Until they drank the pledge of loyalty, both of them had been healthy men. Now they were enfeebled, their bodies poisoned by the the potion.

They were travelling by horse and cart and took a very different route from the road that Glummit had travelled. Although they had seldom been any distance from Black Tor, they had talked to many people over the years and were very familiar with the geography of the islands. They knew enough about Heartsease to keep well away from it and to avoid the roads used by the waggons and carts that travelled to Fowler's Pharmaceuticals. They preferred to choose leafy byways, winding country lanes and sometimes even tracks. It meant that the journey would take longer, but they were old enough to be patient and wise enough to realise that those who travel with most speed are not always the quickest to arrive at their destination.

The first night they rested in a remote farmhouse. It offered plain but wholesome food, and well aired beds. The farmer's wife remarked that they looked ill.

'Nothing like a good rest, country air, plenty of cream and good home baked bread.' she comforted them.

That night Stumble listened to Strug's restless tossings and lay himself in clammy sweat. He knew that it would take more than a good rest and a bit of sunshine to defeat this evil that had gripped them both.

So they travelled on. It was peaceful — with the gentle clop of the horse's hooves, the creak of the cart springs and the crunch of the wheels on gravel. Occasionally they would pause at a duckpond and the horse would stop to lower its head for a drink. There were hedgerows with brilliant flowers, like a patchwork. Scent was in the air, birdsong and the humming of bees. Every time they came to a hill Stumble would dismount from the driver's seat and both brothers would walk beside the horse, soothing, and gently encouraging him up the incline. But their faces were grey now and etched with lines of suffering.

It was a strange contrast. Their journey seemed so peaceful, so idyllic. but they were pressing on as fast as they could reasonably travel. First they had to reach Diamede, then it would take time to arrange a meeting with King Threld. Even if they were able to persuade him to help them, it would all take time and they weren't sure how much longer they could last out. But neither complained, indeed they had little conversation. Their relationship was deep and there was no need for idle chatter.

Their luggage was stored in boxes in the cart behind them, it included the skilful carving of the two stone horses which was intended as a present for King Threld. They also took with them a change of clothes so that they would not look too much out of place in the royal castle.

Late in the afternoon, Stumble saw a speck high in the sky and at a great distance. It was little more than a dot on the horizon and meant nothing to him. He could never have guessed that it was Driftwood making his escape by parachute. He didn't bother to wake his brother who had fallen into an uneasy slumber in the back of the cart

So the horse plodded on. Stumble holding the leather reins loosely between his fingers. On and on they went, the wheels creaking gently as they turned. Within a day or two they would reach Diamede to ask audience with King Threld. A skylark sang above them in the clear air and poppies bloomed in the hedges.

''Tis a fine day.' Stumble murmured to himself. 'Aye, a fine day.'

But his bones ached and every movement of his limbs was an effort.

'What can't be cured must be endured' he muttered.

Back at Dove Cottage, Melody was undoing a tiny message written on the lightest of paper that had been tied to the leg of a white pigeon.

'He's all right!' she called out with relief.

'He doesn't really deserve to be!' grinned her son, the Captain. Inwardly he was as deeply relieved and delighted as his mother. They had all taken a liking to Driftwood and Sorrel.

'How is work going at the ship?' asked Harmony as she brought the tea things out on a tray to the group round the garden table.

'Excellent' replied the Captain. 'We can sail the moment the shields arrive. Without those shields the Daylord would not regard us as prepared.'

'When will it be?' asked Harmony.

'Probably tomorrow' replied the Captain. 'I think you need to go down to Heartsease and warn your friends to be ready.'

'Tell them what a tremendous sight it will be. The sea will be covered with ships like ours as far as the eye can see and the sun will be shining and glinting on the golden shields. 'Twill be a grand day when the four carpenters sound their trumpets. Our flags will be flying, and our fanfares sounding from the decks. What a day to look forward to!'

'Eat your crumpet' said Melody. 'And remember to take Sorrel's toothbrush with you. I want her cabin to be the most comfortable in the whole vessel. She'll deserve that after what she's been through. Take that dress with you. She went off in her old clothes.'

'What has Sorrel been through?' The Captain whispered to Harmony.

'I don't know' she replied. 'You know what Melody's like. She sometimes seems to know what's going to happen before it takes place. Maybe Sorrel hasn't been through it yet.'

'When we're on board ship tonight we'll talk to the Daylord about her' said the Captain 'And about Driftwood too.'

Melody got up from her seat and strolled across to the pond to feed the goldfish. As she came back her face looked a little troubled.

'What is it Melody?' asked Harmony.

'Oh, it's just an impression I had in my mind. I suddenly thought of two stone horses, riding in a cart. Why should they be in the cart, and not pulling it? And they were definitely carved out of stone. It doesn't seem to make sense does it?'

She shook herself impatiently and then relaxed.

'Oh well, the Daylord knows. I'll leave it to him.'

It was opening time at 'The Pillory'. Sorrel was stirring a great pot full of soup in the kitchen when Harry Sleazle started to bawl her name at the top of his voice.

'SORREL! SORREL! By the Black Tor, where is that girl?'

Sorrel ran into the bar and started to apologise, then she stopped and turned to run. There was no escape. Harry Sleazle had reached out one great hairy arm and grabbed her in a vice like grip. There were several customers in the bar and the room was already full of smoke and the smell of drink.

'These 'ere friends of yours is askin' after your 'elth, Sorrel me lovely. Ain't that grand, eh? Ho! Ho! Ho!' He seemed highly amused.

Beyond the bar stood Herbert and Hazy. Herbert was so short that only his face and shoulders showed above the counter.

'That's her' snapped Hazy eagerly. 'That's her.'

'All's well that ends well then.' said Harry cheerfully. He grinned at Sorrel with a leer that revealed the blackened stumps of teeth.

'We ain't known one another long, me girl and we ain't known each other much. But I'll be able to drink yer good 'elth for many a long night to come. This kind friend of yours has paid a tidy sum for you, me girl. Yer ought to be proud to 'ave such friends wot value yer so 'ighly an' all.'

Sorrel struggled frantically in his grasp.

'Please, please, don't send me back' she begged piteously. 'They're cruel. I'd much rather stay here with you Harry. Please, please.'

'Such lack of gratitude, my dear Hazy' said Herbert. 'Such appalling unkindness — and in one so young. It grieves me, I confess it grieves me. When I think of what my poor dear Hazy has had to put up with from you my girl, I can't think why we're prepared to take you back!'

Herbert was spluttering with indignation. But the real reason for his anger was that Harry Sleazle had demanded £50 for Sorrel and Hazy had insisted that he pay up.

'I've struck a good bargain me girl' chuckled Harry delightedly. 'I bet nobody ever got as much out of yer as I 'ave. It were a lucky day for me when you turned up 'ere. Especially as they say, yer a thief an' all —

not to mention a runaway. Fancy that. You with yer nice voice, posh manners an' all. Who'd 'ave thought it of yer?'

He lowered his face from its enormous height so that his red beard almost brushed Sorrel's cheek and his beery breath enveloped her.

''Tis just as well as 'ow yer going 'ome with these nice people 'ere. Cos it wouldn't 'ave done no good to be a stealing 'ere, young Sorrel. The folks round 'ere is very pertikkler. Very pertikkler indeed. They don't like fieves, and they don't like runaways neither! Do yer know wot they does wiv fieves, Sorrel me lass? Listen, and I'll tell yer. They set's 'em free. That's wot they does. They sets 'em free!'

He howled with laughter, and several of the bystanders chuckled grimly. Brushing saliva from his beard, he continued,

'And then, Sorrel — listen to this me girl. When they sets 'em free on the 'illside, do yer know wot they does then, me girl?' He roared with laughter.

'They 'unts the fieves me girl. That's wot they does. They 'unts 'em. Up 'ill and down dale — wiv dogs, and wiv 'orses, and wiv the gentry, all in red. Blood colour, that's wot it is. They 'unts em. 'Tis good fun, ain't it lads? Chasing a fief over the 'ills on a warm summer's night, wiv a moon. And 'im a-stumbling and a-crying and a-'ollering and the dogs a-baying after 'im. We ain't softies like them there folks in 'eartsease.'

'You see, Sorrel' said Herbert kindly. 'We're your benefactors — so generous, so gentle. Such magnanimity my dear Hazy has. I would not have paid so

133

much for you. I tell you frankly I don't consider you worth so much. But Hazy, my dear Hazy — such a spirit sir. A noble soul! Kind to a fault, I assure you, sir. I have often noted it. Kind to a fault.'

CHAPTER 14
SLOBBIT GETS DRUNK

G lummit and Slobbit were playing dominoes in Slobbit's lair — a cellar deep within Threld Manor. They were seated each side of a packing case which they were using as a table. Slobbit enjoyed the game provided he was winning, and Glummit was taking good care that Slobbit won enough games to be well in the lead. His aim was to keep Slobbit in a good humour and to get him drunk.

Fowler had been furious with Slobbit, unleashing upon him all the sarcasm and spiteful malice which he usually kept well under control. Slobbit had effectively been exposed to a blizzard, a cold storm of loathing. He'd been stabbed with icicle words of spite and made to look a complete fool. Not surprisingly, he was now feeling humiliated and resentful.

To the impartial outsider, Slobbit was neither clever, nor likeable. His brilliance lay in his snout, his ability to track down victims. He had fearsome physi-

cal strength, but beyond that, little to arouse admiration. But he was not an impartial outsider. Slobbit was Slobbit. In his own opinion he was a loveable creature of outstanding charm and ability who, given the opportunity, was capable of great achievements. He was certainly worthy enough to rule Diamede or, indeed, any other kingdom whose throne was sufficiently sturdy to carry his weight.

Fowler's withering scorn had angered and depressed him, even if the effect was only temporary. Unable to think clearly enough to offer any defence, he had slunk away like a scolded dog retreating to its kennel. Fowler's anger was all the greater because he knew it was unjustified. The mistake was his, not Slobbit's. He had said too much; he had been careless. Driftwood had been a nuisance, but now he was a positive danger. Within the hour new reward notices were pasted far and wide. The price on Driftwood's head had risen dramatically. He was now worth £5,000 dead or alive. The reward notice claimed that he had attempted to burn Threld Manor to the ground.

It was this sudden increase in Driftwood's value that interested Glummit. He knew that Driftwood hadn't attempted arson. Why then was he suddenly worth so much? What secret had he discovered in Fowler's nest at the top of Threld Manor? So Glummit had loaded himself with as many bottles as he could carry, and had taken upon him the delicate task of comforting and consoling his dear friend Slobbit.

It took far more alcohol than Glummit had expected. Experienced landlord that he was, he knew

how drink could loosen men's tongues and bring them
to make fools of themselves. However, at one stage he
thought that Slobbit must literally have a barrel inside him, so little effect did the drink have. But in the
end Slobbit's tongue began to wag and although his
speech was slurred, Glummit with a mixture of excitement and terror, began to learn of the fearsome
Dreadwater and its effects.

With cunning worthy of Fowler himself, Glummit
played upon Slobbit's high opinion of himself. He fed
the resentment that was already festering in Slobbit's
heart and encouraged dreams of power, riches and
unlimited cruelty. Slobbit's manner became lordly
and expansive and as he rambled on he eventually
shared the secret of his greatest love.

'Shaw her. Shlobbitt shaw her through the what
d'yer call it — the window That'sh it. She made it I tell
yer. Shlobbitt, shaw her.'

'Wot were it like?' asked Glummit cautiously, since
he hadn't the slightest idea what Slobbit was talking
about.

'Delishush' Slobbit hiccoughed and grinned vacantly about him. 'Delishush'.

'Wot were delicious Slobbit?'

When he was drunk, Slobbit had great difficulty in
controlling the movement of his goggle eyes. The
smaller one rolled in the general direction of the
bottle, while the other appeared to be examining his
ear. Speech had become an effort, but he would share
the great secret of his life with his new found bosom
pal. After a struggle he found the words.

'Apple pie' he murmured reverently. 'Makesh apple pie she does. Delishush.'

Glummit was almost beside himself with excitement. He sucked his little moustache and sat in silence for a while as Slobbit snored drunkenly — head on arms amid the dominoes.

It was a pity that he hadn't realised the value of the girl. He had let her leave Dove Cottage because he could see no use for her in his plans. But no matter. Slobbit would be able to find her. The chances were that Driftwood would also be looking for her. And the beauty of it was that £5,000 meant little to Slobbit, whereas unlimited apple pies represented ultimate bliss.

Glummit took a small bottle from an inner pocket and gently but firmly coaxed Slobbit to open his cavernous mouth. His throat gaped like that of a small alligator. While Glummit held Slobbit's great head up, he managed to pour in a generous draught of the concoction. Slobbit's body convulsed, he did a series of kangaroo hops round the room and was taken with a fit of coughing that left him breathless and wheezing. Glummit took him by the arm and steered him out of his lair into the dank corridor and eventually out into the chilly night air.

'Find that there boat again!' he urged. 'Pick up the scent. Apple pie! Remember? The girl the 'umples want. Go get 'er. She's the one wot makes the apple pie. She'll make great pies just for you.'

'Yesh' agreed Slobbit, his mouth drooling. 'Jusht for me. Thatsh a good idea. Shorrel make pie for Shlobbitt.'

The next moment he was gone. His gait was unsteady, but he was no longer so drunk that he was unable to follow a scent. Sometime before dawn Slobbit would track down Sorrel.

As far as Glummit was concerned, they were welcome to each other. He now faced a more difficult task. Nervously he climbed the many flights of stairs to Fowler's secret apartment at the top of the tower. He could hear footsteps inside the room as Fowler paced up and down. Glummit smoothed his sandy hair, licked his moustache and straightened his clothes. Then, summoning all his courage, he raised his hand and knocked at the door.

It was flung open immediately. Fowler's eyes were glinting evilly, his voice grating with pent up fury.

'Two matters' he snarled 'The second shall be first. It's this. Your miserable life hangs by a thread at this moment. The first matter comes second. Find Driftwood.'

'Begging your pardon, Mr Fowler Sir. But if I might just 'ave a few words with you. I think as 'ow I can 'elp you a great deal if you'll just be patient and listen to me.'

Fowler turned his back, swept to the opposite end of the room and swung round facing Glummit, the length of the carpet between them.

'First close the door. Then speak. I see you have news. I trust it's good.'

'Slobbit's drunk' said Glummit bluntly. 'So drunk that 'es gone off 'unting for a girl wot makes apple pie.'

Seeing the look of withering scorn in Fowler's eye, Glummit stretched out an anxious hand.

'Now 'ear me out Mr Fowler, Sir. I ain't wasting words. Remember I'm a man who cares for your interests like they was my own. The point about this 'ere girl is that she an' Driftwood are friends, see? When Slobbit finds the girl, she'll find Driftwood for us. Only it'll make it easier if she don't suss out our little game. If you follow me Mr Fowler, Sir. Let me 'av some Dreirds to go with me, 'an I'll just follow along and bide my time. That Driftwood will show up sooner or later, don't you doubt it. Then I'll nab 'im and bring 'im down to Diamede for you. If I may be so bold, Mr Fowler Sir, you shouldn't stay 'ere not even for one night now. Nasty draughty place with that 'ole in the window. You'll be much more comfortable down at Diamede — and safer too if you get my meaning. Just in case Driftwood were to blurt out anything that might start a revolution.'

Glummit sucked his moustache hard and risked everything.

'Not what you've got anything to 'ide of course Mr Fowler Sir, but suppose for instance that folks were to get to 'ear of that lovely porcelain doll you've got over there. Now of course I know she's just porcelain, ain't she? Or maybe quartz. But she's so real lookin' ain't she? Some folks might almost think she was human once.'

Glummit eyed the bowl of fruit on the bookcase and went on.

'You remember our pub Sir, The Tipsy Goose. We're very patriotic up there at Black Tor you know. Do you know what 'angs over my bed at the Tipsy

Goose, Mr Fowler Sir? Its got a lovely frame 'as that picture. It's a picture of our gracious Queen Threld. Lovely lady that she is — or perhaps I ought to say, was. Strange 'ow much that there image reminds me of 'er. Very strange.'

'Blackmail' hissed Fowler.

'Not at all Sir, not at all, Mr Fowler Sir' protested Glummit. He passed a hand nervously round his collar. 'Pardon me, I'm feeling a bit 'ot like. You ain't got nothing to fear from me, Sir. I'm on your side. I know you could finish me off any time you like. I understand that way of thinking, Sir. But I'm the landlord of the Tipsy Goose that lays the golden eggs — if you'll pardon my little joke, Sir. Let me 'elp look after your interests. Give me a try. You'll see — I'll do it well.'

CHAPTER 15
IN THE STOCKS

'Stop it Hazy! You're hurting me!' cried Sorrel.

Even as Herbert was congratulating his spouse on her noble soul and innate kindliness, Hazy was secretly and cruelly pinching Sorrel's arm under her dress. As Sorrel writhed away from her, Hazy poked her in the middle with a bony finger. She knew just how to do this. Sorrel gasped for breath.

'Come Humple, we're going.'

Hazy marched Sorrel towards the door and the girl struggled with her. Then Hazy took her by the hair and dragged her into the street. Desperately Sorrel fought back. She must have landed a blow because Hazy suddenly lost her temper completely.

'I'll teach you manners my girl. I'll cool you down.'

Hazy was as strong as a grown man. She dragged Sorrel to the horse trough and forced her head down into the icy water.

'Pump Humple.' She commanded in her foghorn voice.

Eagerly Herbert began to crank the pump. A rush of water deluged Sorrel's back and shoulders. Hazy dragged her head up and plunged it down again. Sorrel had never had such a ducking. She couldn't breathe and began to panic.

The men from the pub came out into the street and other people joined them to see what was going on. Nobody seemed to care about the girl. The sweating Herbert pumped while the big woman screamed with rage. It was a sight to behold and the crowd began to laugh. Sorrel could hardly hear the laughter for the rush of water in her ears.

'Let her alone!'

The clear young voice rang out over the din. Herbert Humple leaped back to avoid the punch that Driftwood had aimed at him. Driftwood scooped water from the trough and splashed it all over Hazy. She backed away. Driftwood was blazing with anger.

'Stand back all of you.'

Such was his air of authority that for a moment the crowd backed away from him.

'You should be ashamed of yourselves, all of you! How dare you!'

'Wot's all this then?' Harry Sleazle lumbered forward, long hands wiping the dirty apron around his middle. 'And who might yer be, young cock 'o the walk, giving yerself such airs and throwin' yer weight abaht as if you was Fowler hisself?'

'Never you mind who I am' cried Driftwood. 'You're not to lay a finger on her, do you hear?'

'Huh' snorted Harry. He lumbered toward Driftwood. There was clearly going to be a fight. Delightedly the crowd backed off, leaving Sorrel on the cobbles beside the trough and Herbert and Hazy clutching each other for protection.

The fight was unequal from the beginning. Driftwood knew that his only hope was to keep Harry at a distance and then dash in with lightning blows. He did well and Harry's nose began to bleed. But Harry was too much for Driftwood and soon had him in a crushing bear hug. From then on it was a losing battle. Driftwood rained blows at Harry but the man was so fat that they just seemed to sink into his flesh.

Sleazle could have finished the fight as soon as he chose, but he was shrewd enough to realise that the excitement was drawing a thirsty crowd. So he let Driftwood get the upper hand once or twice — just to sustain the thrills. Then he calmly proceeded to throttle Driftwood with one hand. Once the lad went unconscious Harry dragged him across the cobbles and fastened his legs securely in the stocks. Then he threw water in Driftwood's face to revive him.

'Wot a sight!' he grinned in triumph.

'I know who the lad is!' cried a voice from the crowd. 'I've seen the picture. Fowler wants him dead or alive. Yesterday it was £5 reward, but today its £5,000.'

'Listen my dear good neighbours' said Herbert as an astonished murmur spread round the crowd.

'This dreadful boy broke into our lovely little house, Dunroamin. First class bed and breakfast. He broke

in, threatened us with a red hot poker, locked us in our own room and stole away with our servant girl — this creature Sorrel. See how guilty she looks.'

'Tell them what you did to me!' shouted Driftwood angrily. He was stung by the injustice of what was being said. Herbert Humple smirked, rubbed his hands together and turned his eyes piously towards the sky.

'I did nothing that was not for your best, dear boy. What peace my dear Hazy would have brought to your life. You would not have been in the mess you are in now if you had not resisted the ministrations of my gentle Hazy.'

'That's true enough' muttered Driftwood. 'I'd be dead. Hazy tried to murder me with a chopper.'

Humple shook his head sadly.

'Such delusions. I will not judge him too harshly. We are both very forgiving, my dear Hazy and I. Come now, my good neighbours, let us take our servant girl, and be gone. £5,000 reward, Harry. Shake hands on it. We've made you a rich man. Goodnight, kind Sirs, Goodnight.'

The crowd parted as Hazy dragged Sorrel away. All the fight had gone out of her. She was soaked to the skin and half drowned. It all seemed hopeless. She gazed back piteously at Driftwood. But the next moment Hazy had bundled her into a stage coach and Herbert was clambering up on the box beside the driver. The coachman was whipping up his horses and the coach was rumbling away towards Heartsease.

'Now I'll tell you all about wot's going to 'appen' said Harry.

'First of all, we're going inside for a drink, 'an mark you this. Not one of yer is going to touch 'im unless yer good and drunk first. Get it? I 'ad all the trouble of catchin' the young varmint and I'm lookin' to make a penny or two tonight — not to mention the reward money. Anyone object?'

He gazed fiercely at the crowd, but they were in a good mood.

'It'll be like the old days!' cried a villainous old bystander.

'He's not to be killed neither' dictated Harry sternly. 'Fowler wants 'im dead or alive, but my guess is that 'es worth more alive. Go on in me lads. Fill up yer glasses. I'll just tell the young feller wot 'es got to look forward to.'

He leered down at the helpless Driftwood.

'Now yer know why my pub's called "The Pillory".' he jeered. 'Me and my mates will be drinkin' all evening. When they gets drunk, they gets real nasty. You'll be able to wait for us, I 'ope? I don't see as 'ow you'll be rushing off anywhere. Not wiv yer feet stuck where they is stuck and 'ow they is stuck, if yer get my meanin'.'

Harry slapped his thigh and roared with laughter at his own joke.

'I've got plenty of rotten eggs, and muck from the kitchen. Enjoy the wait young feller, you'll rue the day you punched Harry Sleazle on the nose. An' after we've finished with yer, there's Fowler with his Dreirds. £5,000 reward eh! I wouldn't want to be in your shoes when I 'ands you over to 'im!'

147

With another burst of laughter Harry rolled back into his pub and banged the door behind him. Driftwood struggled frantically. At first he hoped he might be able to wriggle his feet free from the holes, but they were too tightly trapped. There was no way of cutting into the wood; the padlock was large and strong.

Although Driftwood had usually managed to come out on top, he was now well and truly trapped. Time was passing and he was helpless to escape. The wood was unyielding and there was no way he could uproot the device from the cobbled ground. The posts were deeply embedded.

Helplessness was a frightening feeling. His imagination was leaping ahead. There would be no mercy from that drunken crew when they finally lurched out into the street. Despair settled on him and everything seemed hopeless. He sat inert, a hump of misery. His mind went back to Dove Cottage — to Melody and Harmony. How kind they had been — the kindest people he had ever known apart from Chuckle who must have been burned in the fire. Driftwood felt close to tears.

He remembered the conversation about the pearl — how Melody had been so excited to see it. He could almost hear her voice saying 'the pearl brings comfort and peace, not because of what it is, but because of what the Daylord did in another place and another time.'

'Comfort and peace' he thought to himself. 'But what kind of peace can I have in a place like this?' He fished into his shirt and pulled out the leather pouch that hung next to his skin. His fingers delved in the bag and encountered an object the size of a large pea. Amazed, he drew out the pearl and sat looking at it. Did it glow in the dark? Or was it just the reflection of starlight?

Where was the comfort and peace? He remembered how the people from the ship had spoken to the Daylord. And there in the dark, knowing that dreadful things were waiting for him, he closed his eyes and spoke to the Daylord as he clutched the pearl tightly. Nothing happened, but his prayer somehow seemed better than the old one that he remembered Strug and Stumble say with their grey heads bowed at the table — 'Oh thou the unknown who givest light. Give more light.'

'I think that the Daylord must be the one who gives light' he said half aloud. 'And I'm going to hold fast to him and to his pearl.'

Carefully he returned it to its pouch, but it was no longer the size of a large pea. It was now as big as a small marble. And because Driftwood was human and alone with nobody to see, the pearl was also wet with his secret tears.

Down the street at the other end of Grimwald, a horse which had been tearing at the rough grass by the edge of the lane, pricked its ears, tossed its main and gave a gentle whinny.

'Aye lass.' murmured the man who stood waiting, one hand on the bridle. 'We both felt it. 'Tis tears upon the pearl and at last he calls on the Daylord instead of trying to rescue himself. 'Tis time at last! The Daylord says "NOW!"'

The singing from inside the pub was raucous. A sense of detachment came over Driftwood. He was 'for it' and no mistake. But they wouldn't break his spirit. Captive he might be, but coward he need not be. He settled to wait.

In the distance came the faint unhurried clip clop of hooves. Some passer by was leading his horse along the cobbled streets. Maybe he was some belated traveller, a man with a kinder heart than those in the pub. But what could one man do against so many? Besides, the padlock was strong.

'Can you help me please?' Driftwood called softly. The man leading the horse came nearer. He stood silhouetted against the moon.

'Well, well, young Sir' said Chuckle gently. 'So you begin to call on the Daylord at last. 'Tis best to call soon, but late will do better than not at all.'

'Are you the Daylord?' gasped Driftwood eagerly.

Chuckle replied with his characteristic little laugh.

'Not at all young Sir. Just a royal carpenter at your service. Happen as how you need a carpenter just now.'

'You didn't die in the fire then' said Driftwood. 'Somehow I thought you'd escape. But I'm in an awful mess, Chuckle. I don't see how you can get me free. If Harry Sleazle comes out, he's much bigger than you are. You'd better go and hide somewhere. It'd be a comfort to know that you were here, even if you couldn't do anything to help. At least I'd know that I wasn't completely on my own.'

'You know young Sir, it's like as how you remind me of someone else in another time and another place.

Just like yourself, he was wrongfully accused and made a captive by his enemies. But there was no way as how he would hear of being set free. We could have done it, mark my words. Doing it isn't the problem, it's doing it right. We do it as the Daylord wants and when he wants. The when is important you know, young Sir. Anyways, sometimes the Daylord says, "Wait and watch" and sometimes he says "Now!"'

Chuckle grinned and gave another little laugh.

'I tell you this, young Sir, I like it best when he says "Now". And do you know, that's what he did say to Fireflame and me as we were a-waiting down the lane there It came very clearly it did — "NOW"'. He laughed again. 'Oh I like it when he says "NOW"!'

He touched Fireflame gently on the mane and she lowered her head. The harness tinkled as she moved her nose close to the padlock.

'Do you like my mare?' asked Chuckle.

'I never knew you had a horse!' responded Drift-wood.

Chuckle made a clicking noise with his mouth. The mare gently nuzzled at Driftwood's face. He could smell her warm breath. It was sweet like rose blossom.

'This is Fireflame.' Chuckle announced. 'She comes from the royal stables. Aye, young Sir, and a good thing for you that she does, I wouldn't wonder. Show your paces, my girl.'

He led the mare round in a circle and her hooves clattered on the cobbles. Then he backed her towards Driftwood and the stocks that she had already nuzzled.

For one moment she stood, long tail swishing in the cool night air. Then she raised a rear hoof slightly so that only the tip touched the cobbles. Suddenly she struck the roadway sharply with that hoof, grating it across the flints. Yellow sparks shot from the iron of her shoe. A second time the hoof grated, almost like a match being scraped on the side of a box. The third time her head went down and she flung both rear legs upwards. As she did so, she launched a murderous backward kick at the padlock. One hoof struck it fairly and squarely with a shattering impact. Chuckle gazed contentedly at the damage. The padlock had been ripped clean away, and the surrounding wood hung shivered in great splinters. Driftwood was struggling free.

'You know young Sir' said Chuckle gently ''tis said that no injustice stands where the royal horses come riding. Happen as how the old saying may be right enough.'

He glanced towards the rowdy public house.

'Now lad, I've work to do and you must be away. Up into the saddle. Fireflame knows the way.'

Chuckle hurried Driftwood onto his feet and held the stirrup as he mounted the mare. Since Driftwood was on her back, she couldn't travel by another road and another way. There were stones beneath her feet, not stars. Yet never a young man travelled so quickly to Heartsease as did Driftwood. He clung to Fireflame's neck as she pounded across the fields and cleared the hedges and ditches as she sped towards the glowing lights of the bay.

'The Daylord said "Now."' muttered Chuckle to himself.

Stooping, he opened his carpenter's bag, and rummaging among the contents produced a claw hammer. Here was a little round man with a cheery expression, silver grey hair, a green baize apron and a yellow pencil stuck behind one ear. He wasn't exactly a formidable person to look at as he squared his shoulders and marched resolutely towards the Inn.

Arriving at the door he looked up to read the gilt lettered name, 'Harry Sleazle', inserted the claw of his hammer under the board and with one deft twist ripped it from its place. Then he pushed open the door and entered the smoke-filled room which smelt of drink and sweat. The bar was crowded and many of the men were swaying slightly on their feet. Nobody took much notice of Chuckle, but he shouldered his way steadily through till he reached the bar.

''Ere, wot yer think you're a-doing of?' demanded Harry.

He could hardly believe his eyes. A cloth capped stranger with a grey moustache and a pencil behind his ear was calmly nailing Harry Sleazle's own name board to the counter of his bar.

'Stop it, I tell yer — 'oo d'yer think you are a coming in 'ere like this. Wot'yer a-doing of?'

The bangs of Chuckle's hammer had sounded like a call for order. There was sudden silence in the bar.

'Your licence is withdrawn Harry.' said Chuckle. He no longer spoke like a working man. His voice had become strong and stern.

'Listen all of you. "The Pillory" is condemned. There's dry rot everywhere. The whole building is crumbling.'

'I've met some drunks in me time' said Harry 'But you about take the biscuit. Who d'yer think you are? Why, I'm a-going to pull that there moustache of yours right off yer stupid face yer varmint you.'

Harry leaned over the counter and made to grab at Chuckle's jacket. Then suddenly he stopped, locked with a twinge of agonising cramp in his back.

Chuckle pointed upward. 'Dry rot. That's what it is. No mistaking dry rot. Look at that beam!'

Every eye was turned to the main load bearing beam that ran across the ceiling. It had originally been hewn from a single tree and was as thick as a man's waist.

'There's nothin' wrong with that there beam!' roared Harry. Even as he uttered the words, the beam began to sag and plaster started falling from the ceiling.

'"The Pillory" is a condemned building' repeated Chuckle.

At his word, the solid oak door through which he had entered suddenly fell rotten from its hinges and collapsed inwards onto the floor with a great thud and a pile of dust. Panic stricken customers crowded out through the doorway, elbowing, pushing, and falling over each other in their hurry to escape. Then one of the shelves began to give way and there was a tinkling and crashing as glasses and bottles began to shower down.

'Wot's 'appening, I say?' roared Harry again. His back felt better and he leaned forward over the bar which swayed, creaked and began to give way. Chuckle stepped back as Harry Sleazle crashed forward amid the ruins of his own counter. The whiteness of the rot was spreading everywhere. Every wooden barrel was leaking from its joints; every timber was rotting and splitting. Once sturdy benches were crumbling and disintegrating. Heavy stones were starting to fall.

Chuckle hiked Harry to his feet and rushed him out of the Inn. He was only just in time — the heavy granite lintel over the doorway came down with a crash behind him. Roof timbers gave way, and the chimney stack came crashing down through the slates which were falling in clattering showers. Everywhere was dust and confusion. It was like the effects of an earthquake, but the ground was steady.

Outside Harry and Chuckle faced each other with an angry crowd around them. There was no fight. Harry's back had suddenly locked again. He was standing helplessly with one hand digging into the small of his back and his face leaning forward, the red beard jutting from his upraised chin.

From his pocket Chuckle took a plumb-line. Unwinding the twine, he held it close to Harry's chin and allowed it to swing gently before him. Harry stood transfixed, his face wearing an almost comical look of surprise.

'Now' rapped Chuckle. Driftwood would hardly have recognised his voice. 'Sleazle. You have forgotten justice and oppressed the weak. You have lied and cheated. For this you stand condemned. Because you have despised goodness, your own dwelling has become rotten. See the plumb-line. It is straight. You Sleazle, and your cronies have been measured by it and have been found crooked. Just as wood rots, so at my word, a man's bones can rot too.'

As Chuckle said these words another rafter sagged and yet more slates slithered and clattered to the ground.

Harry Sleazle was whimpering now.

'You have been warned, all of you' said Chuckle. He took a pace backward and was gone.

Next morning everyone agreed that it was the drink that had affected them. Harry Sleazle was the loudest of all in asserting that it was all imagination and bad dreams. But for all that, his public house lay in ruins and the stocks in the market place were smashed beyond repair.

CHAPTER 16
APPLE PIE

*G*lummit had sent Dreird horsemen along every main road of the kingdom. It was mid morning, and reports were coming in. Glummit could begin to piece the picture together. He had set up his headquarters in a room at Threld Hall and Dreird secretaries had maps of the kingdom hanging on the walls.

'So' Glummit murmured, thinking aloud 'Mr Fowler 'as taken hisself off to Diamede. 'Es took 'is valuables and precious statue with 'im. Got the wind up 'e 'as, and I don't blame 'im.' Glummit sucked his moustache, and scratched his head.

'Somethin' very queer 'appened at Grimwald in the night. First of all Driftwood was there, and then 'e weren't. Pity that, we nearly got 'im. But we'll 'av 'im soon, never fear. I 'ear that 'arry Sleazle 'ad a funny dream last night. I'd say 'e did. It's a funny kind of dream wot makes yer public 'ouse fall down. P'raps it were an earthquake or somethin'. Anyhow, there's

nothin' there for me, and 'arry don't get no reward for Driftwood neither.' Glummit chuckled to himself and rubbed his hands together with satisfaction.

'At least I know where that there Sorrel is. She's with 'erbert and 'azy 'umple. The Dreirds are definite about that. Took the island ferry first thing this mornin'. Bet they was surprised when Slobbit came up from the engine room and went ashore with 'em. They've got plenty of apples I 'ope. They'll need 'em, that's for sure.' Glummit examined his notebook, licking his finger as he turned the page. His expression was thoughtful.

'The Dreirds 'ave spotted Strug and Stumble. Going to present 'emselves to King Threld they are. Still I needn't worry about that so long as Mr Fowler knows what side 'is bread's buttered on.' Glummit sucked his moustache again.

'Now' he pondered 'what's young Driftwood going to do next? If 'e turns up at Dunroamin, we've got 'im. If 'e makes for Diamedè, we've got 'im again. If 'e tries to contact Strug and Stumble, we're watchin' them. If 'e tries to start a revolution by spillin' the beans about the Dreadwater and Queen Threld bein' turned to quartz — that'd be a nasty business that would. But we've got Dreirds everywhere. If 'es goin' to start a revolution, then 'es got to talk to folks first and as soon as 'e gets up an' starts spoutin' the Dreirds'll nab 'im good an' quick.'

'The best thing 'e can do is to 'ide up somewhere an' keep out of 'arms way. That's what I'd do in 'is shoes. But 'e won't do that, will 'e Glummit me ol' pal? 'E won't do that, because 'es goin' to be worryin' about Strug and Stumble, and 'es goin' to be worryin' about Sorrel!'

'Now there's those two crazy women up at the cottage and that queer lot that's building a ship — not that they'd be much use to 'im anyway. All they do is spout about legends and sing songs and things. We've got a cordon of Dreirds cuttin' the road off if 'e tries to get back to them.'

Glummit poured a measured quantity of liquor into one of Fowler's best glasses.

''Ere's to you, Glummit ol' pal. In a few hours we'll pick up Driftwood somewhere, or else Fowler's Dreirds will catch 'im tryin' to get into Diamede. So what's my next job? I've got to fix Slobbit once an' for all. Fowler don't need 'im now 'es got me. It ought to be easy enough to finish 'im off — 'e ain't got no brain to bother with!'

Slobbit seemed to be getting on very well without a brain. Dunroamin had a new lodger in the front bedroom where Driftwood had narrowly escaped death. The door was damaged where Herbert had used Hazy's chopper to break out of their prison. But Slobbit was totally indifferent to a little damage.

Herbert, sweating profusely, had just arrived at the kitchen door with another wheelbarrow full of apples.

'I really feel, my dear Hazy, that you should speak firmly to our guest' said Herbert. 'His appetite is so ... er ... unreasonable. We shall be completely ruined if he decides to remain for the whole week. How long do you think he'll stay?'

Herbert's voice was pleading. In his small world, Hazy had always been able to solve any problem. He couldn't bring himself to admit that she had met her match in Slobbit.

'The creature takes up so much room. His habits are so ... unpleasant — that plopping noise he keeps making with his mouth. The moment he arrives he goes up and sprawls on our best bed like a great dog. He leaves hairs everywhere — and footmarks.'

There was a bumping noise from upstairs as Slobbit lurched down the main staircase and arrived in the passageway that led to the kitchen. He flung open the door and thrust his leering goggle eyes right up close to Hazy's face.

'Another pie' he demanded. Sorrel who had been baking from the moment they arrived passed a large apple pie to Hazy who proffered it to Slobbit. He seized it from her greedily, grunted with satisfaction and retired to the front parlour.

'He's averaging a pie every two hours' said Sorrel matter of factly. 'I can keep up with that so long as you can get enough flour and fat. We shall need more cloves by this afternoon.'

Hazy who had been strangely silent followed her husband down the garden path and spoke to him near the garden shed.

She lowered her voice and hissed in his ear.

'Weedkiller Humple, weedkiller.'

Herbert was aghast.

'But my dear one, far be it from me to refuse a suggestion which I know is given from a heart of unsullied devotion to my interests. But consider, my delight. There would be his body to dispose of. This creature is not an ordinary guest. He is the chosen servant of Fowler himself. Fowler will surely send Dreirds to find him. Or Fowler might even come himself! What hideous penalty would he mete out to us if we were to dispose of his servant. It doesn't bear thinking of, my beloved. You are overtired, believe me. I understand, but you should not think of such things, let alone whisper them to me. Should the whisper reach Slobbit's master, we would be undone, wretchedly undone!' With a moan of distress Herbert mopped his sweating brow. But Hazy was resolute.

'Plan it, Humple. Plan it.' She grimaced at her husband, put a finger to her lips and coming closer whispered. 'Put the blame on Sorrel. Plan it Humple.'

CHAPTER 17
HARMONY

*H*armony was visiting a friend in Heartsease. They were sitting in the front room of one of the smaller quartz houses in a side street not far from the Pier. The interior walls glowed with a dull amber light. It reminded Harmony of the colour of the hard toffee she used to buy at the Village store.

'Melody says the ship will sail today' Harmony told her friend. 'You need to alert the others. There's not a moment to lose. The Daylord will use the shield light to dazzle the dark powers. Those belonging to the light too bright to be seen will behold the shield light as stars twinkling and aid the victory. New Diamede shall shine forth in splendour. It will be the central jewel surrounded by the glory of the shields as they sparkle and glitter like brilliant gems in a coronet. This is what the Daylord has promised us through the messages of his servants. We must hurry though, for the time is short and what is to be will be. Fowler's rule will end and the quartz city will melt away.'

Tanya nodded in agreement. 'I'm leaving everything' she said. 'I've known for a long while that it will all be washed away, but some of my friends are doubtful about it. I only hope they'll be ready in time.'

'What about Bel?' asked Harmony.

Tanya shook her head sadly. 'Poor Bel. She's become so taken up with her friends. She can't believe that I was ever young myself, or that I understand. I think that sometimes it's almost as if she hates me. When I tell her that the houses are going to melt like ice, she just taps her forehead. She thinks I'm completely mad.'

'Perhaps I could talk to her' suggested Harmony.

Bel's mother nodded eagerly and went to the door of the room. Standing at the bottom of the staircase she called Bel's name. Eventually there was the clomping sound of someone coming downstairs and Bel arrived in the doorway.

She was in a condition of carefully contrived untidiness. Harmony knew that this was 'The Look.' Most young people in Heartsease dressed this way. It was important that shoes did not match, and that sleeves should be frayed. Harmony wasn't bothered by Bel's appearance; she understood about fashion. But from the start it was clear that Bel was in one of her moods.

'Swog it, Mother' she complained. 'Can't you ever leave me alone! Oh, it's you Harmony. Those swog pigeons of yours woke me up in the middle of the night. Can't you train them to be a bit more quiet? I don't know why Mother agreed to have them to start with.'

'Bel' said Harmony urgently 'The ship sails today. You will be ready, won't you. It's all going to be tremendously exciting.'

'Your idea of excitement don't get to me, Harmony. I've got to get my hair done this afternoon. You should see the new hairdresser, he's skoozle.'

'I know hair is important' said Harmony tactfully. 'And I know we've been waiting so long for the ship to sail that some of you have got bored about it. But it really is sailing this time. Please come with us!'

Bel yawned. 'It's swog inconvenient!' she groaned. 'I'll think about it, but don't count on me. The thought of pulling one of those oars don't get to me at all.'

'Don't you want to see New Diamede?' asked her mother with just a hint of irritation in her voice.

'Oh New Diamede would be skoozle all right. If it ever happens. But my friends say it's all myths and legends. Four carpenters and all that swog stuff. I told you, it don't get to me. I'm drifting off now, Mother. Bye Harmony.'

The front door banged and she was gone.

Shortly afterwards Harmony left the house. She made her way down towards the Pier. A group of youngsters were lounging outside a dice hall. Dice was a speciality at Heartsease. The game was played with huge quartz dice, which were rolled in a large transparent barrel or drum known as the Skoozle bin. A lot of money changed hands during the games. This was the pastime that had been Sorrel's downfall.

Harmony was conscious that she must look drab and old fashioned to this group of youngsters. Her

shoes matched. Her sleeves weren't frayed. Her hair hung gracefully whereas to be skoozle, it should have been shaped into two greasy horns.

'Swog Dlo Nammow' said a voice. Harmony knew Dlo Nammow was backslang for old woman. She pretended not to have heard and hurried on her way. There was a patter of shoes on the pavement behind her. The group were following her.

Another voice began to sing mockingly, 'Washed away, washed away, won't it be skoozle when we're washed away!'

There were more jeers and nasty comments from the crowd. Harmony forced herself to walk steadily, though she was timid by nature and the situation was beginning to get rather scary. Suddenly a lad brushed passed her knocking her arm roughly. He cut in and walked ahead of her with a pronounced waddle. This was hardly fair, for Harmony was certainly not overweight.

'You're Taf, Taf, Taf' called a boy's voice.

Then they were all round her. Edging her towards the stone wall where the waves washed against the promenade.

'Fancy a swim Dlo Nammow?' leered one of the bullies, pushing his face towards Harmony and blowing up his cheeks.

'Swog it, leave her alone!' It was Bel's voice from the back of the crowd. 'She's a friend of my Mother's.'

'She's a friend of Mummsie's, she's a friend of Mummsie's' several voices chanted the mocking refrain.

'She thinks she's better than us!' accused someone. 'She doesn't belong down here!' said another. 'She's one of the ship people. Let's see if she floats!' exclaimed a third.

One step backward, and Harmony would fall off into the surging water below. She wasn't likely to drown, she could swim well enough. But she would be soaked — this day of all days when the ship was about to sail.

Harmony found that in this tight corner, her usual timidity was draining away from her. She faced the bully and took a step forward. Just at that moment there was a flutter of wings and one of the pigeons from Dove Cottage landed on her shoulder. She'd made pets of all of them, so this didn't seem unusual to her. They often came to her in this way.

Her mind was so preoccupied with the bully in front of her, that she raised her hand more out of unconscious habit than as a deliberate gesture. He backed away and she stepped forward again. Terror was glazing his face. Harmony was suddenly conscious of the heavy weight of the bird as it hopped onto her wrist. None of her own pigeons had ever been so dazzling white. There was not one grey feather on the hawk whose claws fastened gently but firmly upon her sleeve. This was not one of her pigeons! Its feather's were whiter than those of a swan, it's size larger than a peregrine falcon. It looked terrible to the crowd. Suddenly it spread its mighty wings and craned its beak towards the bully's nose. There was a panic stricken stampede as the crowd scattered this way and that.

Next moment the bird was flying rooftop high, then higher still, then it was slashing down, like the flashing blade of a scimitar. It had only one target — the bully — and there was no escape for him. Had the falcon used beak and claws, his face would have been scratched to ribbons, but there was moderation even in anger. The bird wrapped its great wings round the bully's head and pushed its strong claws into the nape of his neck. With a yell and a splash the bully hit the water, then the bird soared high again, its eagle eyes searching for another victim. None were to be found. The crowd had scurried away like mice before a predator. Harmony walked away, head erect, determined not to run.

'Don't waddle!' she admonished herself. 'Whatever you do walk gracefully!'

High above her like a speck in the azure sky, the great hawk wheeled and circled. Only as she returned to Dove Cottage did it turn to windward and glide down towards the mast of the Captain's ship.

CHAPTER 18
CALM

*I*n one way, Slobbit's arrival had been a great benefit to Sorrel. As pie maker in chief, she was privileged and protected. Had Slobbit not been there, there is no telling what cruelties Herbert and Hazy might have perpetrated to punish her. But any thought of punishment or revenge was obliterated by the mountainous presence of the six fingered giant. Sorrel had deft fingers and provided Herbert kept bringing the apples, she knew she could soon get ahead of Slobbit's appetite. By mid morning she was out in the garden hanging washing on the line.

She heard the gate click and looked up to see the stooping figure of a lean grey haired man. He was carrying a carpenter's bag and was wearing a blue baize apron.

'Good morning my dear' he said cheerfully. 'Would there be any knives to grind, drains to be cleaned, or odd jobs to be done?'

Sorrel shook her head.

'I doubt it very much, but if you like to come on up to the house, it's best that you ask for yourself.'

Now it happened that Hazy had a delight in sharp tools. When Herbert used the steel to sharpen the carving knife, he always managed to blunt it. It was Herbert who made a great rattle and clatter, but it was Hazy who by rubbing the blade on the back door step, gave it what edge it had. So the offer of 'knives to grind' had some attraction for her. Also she thought she recognised in the carpenter one of those elderly tradesmen of whose kind she approved.

Hazy liked honest, reliable, useful, kind hearted old men. She appreciated them because she had always been able to persuade them to do far more odd jobs for much less money than they had originally agreed. Shrewd bargaining, and artful dealing were some of Hazy's joys in life. She had even been known to buy things she neither wanted nor needed, simply because she had haggled for them and bought them at a ridiculously low price.

Then again, there were many jobs around the garden and house that Herbert was neither willing nor able to do. Herbert had no head for heights and was useless with tools. His efforts to mend things usually left them in a worse state than before.

So the carpenter, who gave his name as 'Calm,' started work at Dunroamin. He fixed the gutter, pruned a fruit tree, mended the fence and split a great pile of logs for the fire. About midday Sorrel came down to the garden shed with a tray. Calm laid down his axe and came toward her. She carried the tray into the shed and put it on the bench.

'I'm ashamed to bring you this really' she said. 'It's only a piece of bread and butter and a mug of tea. That's all Hazy wants you to have. But ...' she dived into the pocket of her apron and produced an apple and a hunk of cheese 'perhaps you can manage to eat these as well. I don't want any lunch myself. I don't eat much and I'm not feeling hungry. Do take it please. I'm sure you must have worked up an appetite.'

The old man eyed her gravely.

'Thank you' he said 'Please stay and talk to me a moment. I'd really like to know more about you.'

'I mustn't be long' said Sorrel. 'I shall get into trouble. But perhaps if you eat slowly, I can say I waited to bring back the mug and the tray.'

So while the old carpenter took his lunch break, Sorrel perched on top of an upturned box and chatted to him. She found it easier to talk to him than to anyone she had ever known before. Her tongue seemed to run away with her and all the while his kindly eyes rarely left her face. She told him about her escape and about Driftwood and the terrible events at Grimwald.

'I'm so worried about him' she said anxiously. 'All morning I've been racking my brains to think of a way of getting help. But the world seems full of cruel people and they have all the power. The kind ones like the people with the ship, seem so helpless and — sort of useless really. I mean they're more interested in legends and singing songs than they are in people. Perhaps that's unfair, but that's what it seems like to me.'

Calm sliced the cheese with his big pocket knife and arranged the pieces neatly between the two halves of his piece of bread.

'What if I were to tell you that the Daylord cares about you?' he asked.

'I shouldn't believe you' said Sorrel bluntly. 'I don't think there can be a Daylord. If there was, he'd do something to help Driftwood.'

'But he wants to help you' said the carpenter.

Sorrel tossed her hair impatiently. 'I don't matter. There's no reason to worry about me. I can take care of myself. In any case, I'm not worth bothering about!'

'Who says so?' asked Calm, eyeing her over the edge of his mug of tea.

'Hazy says so all the time' sighed Sorrel. 'I used to think she was wrong. I used to tell myself that I was pretty and that if I had a chance to get my hair done properly, and have some decent clothes to wear, I'd be O.K. But I'm always getting into trouble. Hazy says I'm ugly and stupid and I expect that she's right.'

Sorrel paused and then, as if finding relief in sharing with someone, went on.

'You know, when I met those people at Dove Cottage, I felt awful. I just didn't belong somehow. They made me feel cross because they were so good and kind and I wasn't. I gambled you know. That's how I lost the money and came here in the first place.' She sniffed and angrily dabbed at the corner of her eye.

'I told lies and got myself into all sorts of scrapes. I'm not their sort at all. If there is a Daylord he wouldn't be interested in someone like me.'

Calm sat looking at her gently, his eyes seeming to read everything in her heart.

She gulped and looked down. Her hair fell round her face. Then she nodded to herself and looked up towards him.

'You might as well hear the rest. One afternoon I gambled away everything that was left from the money my old nurse left me. I was desperate. Then I saw this purse on the counter at the grocer's. It belonged to this lady. I didn't know her then, but I recognised her as soon as I saw her. It was the one they called Harmony from Dove Cottage. She was buying some shopping down at the grocer's, and her purse was lying there.' Sorrel sniffed again. 'She never saw me, she never knew. I thought I'd win next time. Then I could take her purse back and say I found it lying in the street or something. But of course I lost. So I spent the last coins on the ferry to the island and came to live here.

Now you know the worst about me. So you see, the Daylord wouldn't care about me. He probably sent me to the Humples to be punished — and now I've got Slobbit demanding apple pies into the bargain!'

She grinned and tried to pull herself together.

'Well, I must be off, or there'll be more trouble.'

Calm hardly seemed to have heard what she was saying. He had put his hand into the pocket of his apron and now he was steadily counting a pile of coins onto the bench. He reached into his pocket again and pulled out a lady's purse. Sorrel gasped and her face went pale. She put a hand to her hair, then turned

away from him. Her shoulders began to quiver as her body shook in silent misery. After a few moments Calm produced a blue handkerchief with big white spots on it.

'Have a blow' he suggested.

She raised her face towards him, tears streaming down her cheeks.

'How did you know?' she whispered 'That's the very purse — but I threw it into the sea. That's the precise amount of money.'

Calm nodded gravely.

'Very likely' he said gently 'But the Daylord told me to show all this to you and to ask you what I should do. There's enough money here to help you to escape if that's what you want.'

Sorrel shook her head indignantly.

'Of course not!' she exclaimed. 'I'm not going to make the same mistake twice. I'm fed up with lying and gambling and scheming. Hazy can beat me black and blue and I'll make apple pie for Slobbit till he bursts, but I'm not running away from things any more.'

'I could take the purse back to Harmony' suggested Calm. 'I clean windows at Dove Cottage every week. They know me well.'

'Please do that!' begged Sorrel. 'And please tell them to ask the Daylord to rescue Driftwood. I'll stay here and take my punishment if you do that.'

Calm put down his empty mug. 'You don't have to take your punishment, child' he said gently. 'The Daylord dealt with that long ago, in another place and another time.' Just at that moment Hazy bawled Sorrel's name and with an anguished gasp Sorrel snatched up the tray and fled.

In the early morning Fireflame brought Driftwood to the beach where his dinghy was hidden among the sand dunes. No sooner had he dismounted than the horse had cantered away. Driftwood felt at a loss. What was he supposed to do? He thought of Strug and Stumble pressing on to Diamede. He had been slower than Glummit to recognise the doll in Fowler's apartment because his mind had been busy with other things. But by now he had realised that the Queen must have been tricked into drinking the Dreadwater. If this was so, it was probable that there was no King Threld at Diamede. In which case Strug and Stumble would be in grave danger. On the other hand Sorrel was much nearer his own age so maybe he should rescue her so that they could go to Diamede together.

He was beginning to realise the importance of the pearl as his link with the Daylord. So, standing by the boat, he fished it out to view it in the early morning light. It was now the size of a small bird's egg.

'What am I to do?' he pondered aloud.

As he asked, he was conscious of a gentle pressure that the pearl was exerting on his palm. He swung his hand towards Threld Manor — there was no pull. He swung it towards Heartsease — no pull. He swung it back towards Dove Cottage, but still the pearl lay dormant. It was the same when he waved his arm in the direction of the island and Dunroamin. But when he pointed towards Diamede, the gentle pressure on his

hand was unmistakeable. Driftwood grunted to himself as he returned the pearl to its pouch.

'I hope I've got it right.' he thought as he set about preparing the dinghy to sail. As the sun rose for a new day, the boat was already out in the waters of the bay bound for Diamede. This journey Driftwood must make alone.

Dreirds had repaired the damage done to Fowler's apartment. By mid morning Glummit had returned to search for anything that might be useful to him. He soon realised that Fowler had cleared the room. But standing in the middle of the desk was a large bottle of vintage wine. By it lay a gilt edged card.

'For my dear friend Glummit. Here's to our lasting partnership. Your grateful ally, Fowler!'

There was also a corkscrew. Glummit stood looking at the bottle, head slightly on one side. He licked his moustache thoughtfully. Then he moved round, viewed the bottle from another angle and summoned a Dreird.

'Uncork it for me, an' be quick about it' he ordered.

The Dreird used the corkscrew that was lying so conveniently close to the bottle. The cork came out easily. Glummit carried it to the window to get a good look at it. The surface glistened slightly. Glummit, who knew all about corks, was careful not to get too close.

'The artful ol' villain!' he muttered to himself.

'Barrier cream, that's what it is. Protects the cork from the liquid it do. Now that's clever Mr Fowler, but not quite clever enough.'

With great care he returned the cork to the bottle.

Once it was securely in place he rubbed at it so that the mark made by the corkscrew was hardly visible — not that he expected the next customer to be particularly observant.

CHAPTER 19
MURDER AT DUNROAMIN

'**W**e're going to have a party this evening, Sorrel' said Herbert. 'I've invited Madam Dubarry from the grand house up the street. Mr and Mrs Whimple and Miss Whimple from Orchard Cottage. Captain Sprigg from the coastguard's house. I've ordered a large ham, pies and puddings. Oh such a feast!'

Sorrel was amazed. Parties were unheard of at Dunroamin. She had never known Herbert in such a genial mood.

'It's to celebrate Mr Slobbit's arrival!' Herbert explained rubbing his sweaty palms together. 'Do you know what gave me the idea? I'll let you into the secret. It was this lovely present.'

Herbert reached down into a corner of the kitchen and produced a large bottle.

'This arrived this morning by special delivery. One of those quiet gentlemen they call Dreirds brought it up to our house. Such an honour! A visitor from Threld

179

Manor. There was a card with it. Read it Sorrel. It says, "To my dear friend Slobbit." Such a noble style of greeting. Just think! Dear Mr Slobbit is the personal friend of the great Mr Fowler! To think that such an honoured guest is staying at our humble home. We shall present the bottle at the party this evening.'

'He'll drink the lot at one gulp' said Sorrel bluntly. 'I don't see the point of inviting people to watch him. It will be a revolting sight what with that squelching noise he makes with his mouth!'

Herbert Humple wagged an admonishing finger at her, but didn't seem greatly angered.

'My dear generous Hazy thinks differently' he said. 'She lacks your hard nature, Sorrel. You know that my sweet one is soft and tender. "Humple" she said to me, these were her very words, Sorrel. "Humple" she said "show kindness." That's what we are resolved to do, Sorrel my girl — and in front of many witnesses — ahem — I mean good friends. We shall show kindness. We shall be generous. No expense will be spared. We shall celebrate together this very evening. Now girl, get to work and polish the front parlour.'

It was perfectly true that a Dreird had brought the bottle of expensive wine from Threld Manor. Glummit had sent it in Fowler's name. However the arrival of the bottle had given Herbert and Hazy an opportunity.

Although he was useless at most things, Herbert was a talented forger and had spent the early part of the afternoon working on a duplicate bottle. Tongue sticking out of the corner of his mouth, he had sat hunched over a table, laboriously checking and rechecking. Often picking up a magnifying glass to make sure that his work was perfect. When he had finished, two identical bottles stood on the table before him. The one from Threld Manor Herbert believed to be full of delicious vintage wine.

The other bottle was empty at first. Then Hazy Humple arrived. She had been busy mixing the poison — which was difficult. The dose must be lethal. Slobbit was enormous and would take a lot of killing. But the poison must not act too quickly because Hazy didn't want her guests to be upset. On the other hand the taste must be reasonable because Slobbit would spit it out all over everyone if he disliked the flavour.

Hazy had abandoned the idea of weedkiller and had chosen a more subtle poison — one that she'd stored away years earlier. She had obtained this poison and learned its secrets in her early years of marriage to Herbert. As a youth Herbert had been very annoying and his life had hung in the balance on more than one occasion. However up to now Hazy had shown restraint. Truth to tell Herbert had no real love for Hazy either, but by constant flattery he had managed to keep on the right side of her.

When at last Hazy was satisfied with the smell and colour of the mixture, she brought it to Herbert who, with the dexterous use of a small funnel, succeeded in filling and corking the bottle without spilling any on the label. Herbert leaned back and surveyed his work with satisfaction.

'Shall we sample the genuine bottle, dear Hazy?'

'Not till he's dead, Humple, not till he's dead.'

So Herbert hid the genuine bottle away in the cellar. It was the duplicate bottle of poison that he showed to Sorrel.

The plan was simple. In front of witnesses Sorrel would ply Slobbit with drink. When he died, the first suspicion would fall upon her. Since the bottle apparently came from Threld Manor, people might suspect that Fowler had a hand in the deed. But this being the case, Herbert knew that they wouldn't dare to pursue enquiries any further.

Once again if Dreirds came from Threld Manor to investigate, then Herbert and Hazy would testify that Sorrel had poisoned Slobbit because she was unwilling to keep making him apple pies. To Herbert it seemed like the perfect murder plan. Nobody cared much about justice these days. So long as a culprit was found and was punished, that was all that mattered.

Slobbit was pleased with the idea of a party. It seemed obvious to him that a noble creature like himself deserved the homage of the whole village. What more natural thing was there than a celebration to mark his arrival?

Hazy made Sorrel dress in a prim maid's uniform for the occasion. Her apron was clean and stiffly starched. Towards evening, the guests began to arrive: Captain Sprigg, a rather florid old gentleman and Mrs Whimple with husband and pallid looking daughter in attendance. Madame Dubarry brought her nephew who proved to be able to play the violin — so there would be music and song.

Hazy gave Slobbit what she called 'the place of honour'. It was her most comfortable chair, arranged in a convenient corner near the fireplace. She cunningly contrived to place tables and screens in such a manner that her guests were spared the more disgusting of Slobbit's eating habits. Sorrel had been equipped with an extensive supply of clean flannels and towels with which to mop up the mess at frequent intervals.

'Your duty' explained Herbert 'is to keep Slobbit happy this evening. After all, it is his party. Who knows whether he will ever have another one. Let's all give him a good time. My dear Hazy wants him to be kept happy at all costs, Sorrel. At all costs.'

Other guests arrived and the celebration went on until late. Captain Sprigg had a fund of stories which he judged to be very funny. He laughed at himself with great good humour. The food was superb. Hazy knew how to prepare a feast when it suited her — as Driftwood had discovered. The tables groaned under lavish delicacies. People played cards. Miss Whimple who had a pleasant voice sang and Madame Dubarry's nephew accompanied her on his fiddle. Slobbit ate steadily on and on. It was a pleasant change from his customary life of tracking, hunting and lying out under bushes in the cold. He was contented.

In the late evening Herbert took Sorrel down to the cellar and gave her explicit instructions. Then he took his stand in the middle of the parlour and, clapping his greasy palms together, he called for everyone's attention.

'Ladies and gentlemen. This is a very auspicious evening in the life of our little community. As you know, we are honoured to have a very special guest staying in our village — none other than the honourable, the noble Mr Slobbit of Threld Manor. He's the friend and trusted companion of the great Mr Fowler. This noble man has sent a presentation bottle of wine to crown our celebrations this evening. I shall call on you all to stand and drink a toast together before we go our different ways.'

At this point Sorrel entered with a large iced cake, topped with lighted candles. Each guest was served a small portion. Slobbit behind his screen was given the other half of the cake. He blew the candles out, ate them first and then proceeded to finish off the cake.

Then Sorrel returned bearing full glasses on a silver tray for Herbert's guests, and also the special bottle reserved for Slobbit. Hazy passed her guests glasses filled with ordinary cheap wine while Sorrel, on Herbert's instructions, approached Slobbit's chair.

Herbert took great care that everyone's attention was focused on the presentation. Sorrel curtsied to Slobbit as she had been told to do. Then she gave him the bottle. Law and order was fairly primitive on the island. Most of the inhabitants were fairly simple minded in their thinking. It would be easy enough to settle the blame for Slobbit's death on Sorrel. After all, everyone saw her give him the drink.

Slobbit fell for it without any trouble. His good friend Fowler had sent him a bottle. Well and good. Ripping out the cork with his teeth, he spat it out into the fire. Then leaning back his head, he gulped and guzzled till he'd emptied the entire contents. Not long after, Hazy helped her guests into their coats and waved them from the house. By the time she returned, Slobbit was in a stupefied slumber. Herbert and Hazy helped him upstairs and locked him in the bedroom.

'My beautiful Hazy' crooned Herbert, 'my dear delightful creature, how clever you are. He'll never wake again. Our troubles are ended!'

Sorrel, who suspected nothing, cleared away in the kitchen and, at about 2 a.m. crawled into bed and fell asleep. At 3 a.m. there was the most terrible roar and shriek from Slobbit's room. Then utter silence. Down in the cellar Herbert and Hazy sat facing one another. The real bottle from Threld Manor stood between them, and in front of them two of Hazy's finest glasses. Although they really had plenty of money, they were so mean that neither of them had ever drunk an expensive wine. The bottle from Threld Manor looked very impressive, and they were looking forward to sampling it. As the shriek echoed from upstairs Herbert poured the drink into their glasses.

'Your very good health my dear, lovesome, sweetheart' cried Herbert. Gleefully the two conspirators clinked glasses and raised them to their lips.

'To absent friends' said Herbert.

Slobbit's cry brought Sorrel running out of her room, a lighted candle in her hand. The door was still broken, so she pushed the candlestick through the aperture. She could see Slobbit's body lying across the floor near the door. He had fallen on his back and one great goggle eye glinted in the candlelight. There was no sign of life.

Ugly suspicions were forming in Sorrel's mind. She ran to the Humples' door and knocked. Nobody answered. After a moment she tried the handle and entered the room. The bed had not been slept in. Where could they be? She began to search the lonely house, calling their names. The house felt eery and empty. Slobbit was dead upstairs and fear was beginning to grip her. She called aloud and more anxiously and searched downstairs. Eventually she thought of the cellar.

When she opened the door she saw a light shining down below. 'Oh, there you are!' she cried in relief. She hurried down the steps to where Herbert and Hazy sat with the bottle between them and glasses raised to their lips.

'Please come quickly! I think Slobbit has been taken very ill. He may be dead. Please hurry!'

She stopped at the foot of the cellar steps. Neither Herbert nor Hazy moved. Suddenly afraid, Sorrel crossed the stone flags of the cellar. The lamplight made their features even more grotesque than usual. But their eyes were sightless and unmoving. No breath passed their lips. Hazy's mouth was pursed in grim disapproval. Herbert's mouth was half open as though he was still babbling on, but he was silent now — for ever. The two figures were not made of flesh; they were solid quartz.

Sorrel was alone. The night was pitch dark and an unknown horror lay upstairs. She wished she could faint. Gasping and whimpering she made her way up the cellar steps and hurried back into the kitchen.

Suddenly the garden gate clicked. Sorrel seized the same meat cleaver with which Hazy had prepared to murder Driftwood. She backed into a corner of the kitchen away from the door. Whatever was coming to get her, she would fight till the last. She wanted to scream aloud, but instead she bit her lip and swung the cleaver in her hand. The back door swung open, and a tall figure stooped in the darkness.

'Don't you come a step closer' gasped Sorrel. 'I'll chop you to pieces if you come near me.'

'Oh, my child!' said Calm from the doorway. 'Oh, my poor child.'

CHAPTER 20
THE SHIP

At first Calm let Sorrel cry — she needed to let out some of the emotion. After a short while she began to feel better and told him about Slobbit lying dead upstairs. He went to check things over and returned a few minutes later with a grave face.

'Slobbit's gone' he said. 'The poison wasn't strong enough. It looks as though he was furiously angry and in great pain. He's wrecked the room, bent the iron bars apart and escaped.'

'Why didn't he come down here?'

Calm smiled gently down at her. 'I'm a royal carpenter. I travel by another way from another time. Often the Daylord in his wisdom restrains me and will not let me help. But when I'm allowed to come near, then there is a wall of protection that shelters from Slobbit and from all other night terrors. Slobbit wouldn't know that I was here, but he would be suddenly terrified and afraid of this house. So he has escaped into the night.'

189

'I feel so safe with you!' said Sorrel.

'Yes, my child, but there are yet dangers to come. I must find companions for you to guard you. The Daylord will call me to other places and other times. I cannot always show my power to protect you.'

Calm went on to explain how some enemy from the mainland had attempted to use Dreadwater to turn Slobbit to quartz. Calm said that he didn't think it could be Fowler himself but probably a man called Glummit who may have seen Slobbit as a rival. Unfortunately for them, Herbert and Hazy had switched bottles. Their poison had not been strong enough to finish Slobbit off, but it had made him very ill. In turn they had drunk the Dreadwater and become its victims.

'The difficulty now is that Slobbit will believe that you hurt him, Sorrel. He isn't all that bright and he will suppose that since you were the one who gave him the bottle, you must have been the one who wanted him out of the way.'

'But I cooked him lots of apple pie!' protested Sorrel.

'Yes, but even Slobbit isn't going to fancy apple pie if he thinks there may be poison in it. No, we have to keep you safely out of Slobbit's way until this whole thing is over. I know the people who will care for you, but you must find them for yourself. That is what the Daylord says to me. I am to take you across the island, but then you must find out what to do.'

Sorrel hurried to get changed. Now that Calm was there, the house was no longer frightening. She left her servant's apron behind, along with everything else that would remind her of Dunroamin. Calm let her out into the first light of dawn when, over the moors, there were streaks of pink which tipped the fleecy clouds.

''Twill be a fair day, you'll see' he promised.

In the lane his horse, Spindrift, was quietly grazing. He seemed pleased to see his master. Calm swung Sorrel up into the saddle in front of him and they set off together. For a while they rode in silence except for the swift drumming of the horse's hooves on the springy turf. Then they clattered down a slope to a place where Spindrift's hooves struck sparks from flints and up again to the crest of a hill. Sorrel marvelled at the strength and speed of the creature that carried them. For miles they cantered and the horse neither sweated nor panted nor slackened its pace. The cool morning air rushed past her ears and the first birds were singing high in the sky. In the distance she could see the deep ocean and darkness over the water.

''Twill be a fine day, Sorrel, a fine day' comforted Calm, just as he had said before. But this time he slowed down and swung her from the saddle to the ground. Before she was fully aware of what was happening, he and Spindrift had disappeared.

The path beside her led toward the cliffs. She presumed that she was meant to go this way as there was no other track to follow. The dawn was glorious. It took her some time to clamber down into the bay, but before long she was carrying her shoes and walking barefoot. The cool sand squeezed up between her toes, and her feet sunk into the sand of the dunes. The tang of seaweed was in her nostrils and she felt dried seaweed brittle beneath her feet.

She went on, until suddenly she heard the sound of voices and froze with fear. Her first thought was that they were Dreirds. Dropping flat on the ground she crawled forward till she could see the group of people more clearly.

A big bonfire was blazing on the beach and a cheerful group of people were breakfasting around it. Further out in the calm waters of the bay lay the ship that she'd seen when she first came ashore with Driftwood. There was a change however. All along the side of the vessel were shields. They were round, and highly polished and even in the light of dawn, they shone like solid gold.

'It's the ship people!' thought Sorrel. She was about to rush forward, when they began to get to their feet and join hands around the fire. She watched as they started singing one of their strange songs about the Daylord.

Sorrel felt uncomfortable. Part of her wanted to join the safety of that happy group, but another part of her was struggling with the past. She had lived a long while with the Humples. Apart from Driftwood, she had never made any close friends. She felt embarrassed about her past life and about the kind of questions she might be asked if she joined them. Worse still would be the experience of finding everyone so dreadfully kind and understanding. She might get the kind of creepy feeling that she'd had when she was at Dove Cottage.

Then she hit on an idea. If she could get to the boat without being seen, she might be able to stow away on board. She would certainly be safe from Slobbit and if they were going to Diamede, then she might be able to join up with Driftwood again. She felt that with Driftwood as a friend, she might be able to get used to going to the meetings and singing the songs.

Leaving her shoes behind, she kept low among the dunes and crept down to the sea edge. The water was calm but bitterly cold and the waves swished gently against the sand. The group round the fire were still singing lustily, their attention taken up with other things. The beach shelved rapidly. Sorrel lowered herself into the water without any tell tale splashes and struck out gamely in the direction of the great ship. She was confident in the water and the exercise warmed her.

Eventually she reached the ship and swam round the prow of the vessel so that she could approach it from the seaward side. Treading water, she moved round to a stout hawser by which the craft was anchored. It ran upwards to a porthole. Hauling herself out of the water, she clambered up the rope. It was a struggle to climb over the edge of the vessel, but with an effort she made it — and tumbled over the side onto the cedar planking of the deck. She couldn't see a sentry on board and was too out of breath to notice the great white bird which flew from the rigging as she arrived.

First she must hide somewhere. She was used to hardship and reasoned that she could manage for a couple of days without food, especially if she could

get some rainwater to drink. In the distance she could hear the sound of singing on the beach. They were still enjoying themselves. She was safe for a while and crept down into the main deckhouse.

This great cabin wasn't furnished with tables or chairs. Instead there were many rugs, cushions and hanging curtains. It was all very beautiful and Sorrel recognised that almost everything was handmade needlework or weaving. There was a great deal of rich embroidery and many beautiful pictures and patterns. The day was still dim, but the pink glow of the rising sun cast shafts of light through the portholes and Sorrel would have been fascinated to examine the tapestries and furnishings. But she was still seeking a safe hiding place.

The smell of the ship was a surprise. It was almost a scent or fragrance. Cedar wood, old leather, dried rose petals, musk, and other subtle scents mingled with the fresh sea air. There was no staleness, no smokiness, no smell of rotten wood or engine oil. On this great cabin rested a peace that felt almost like a companionable presence — the kind of silence that exists between loving friends who trust one another completely. Yet Sorrel consciously resisted that feeling of security.

'I don't belong here!' she told herself.

Descending the companionway, she found herself on a larger deck where the rowers would sit on benches. Here the breeze was blowing through. She could imagine men bending to the oars, but there was no sign of chains or leg irons to secure any galley slaves.

The Ship

Fore and aft were more cabins. She took a ladder which led down into the darkness and eventually felt her way deep into the lower part of the ship. She realised that she must now be well below the water line. What faint light there was came from a small ventilation shaft above her. She was just able to make out a hatch in the floor and found that she could prise this up with her fingers. For the first time there was a dank and stale smell. She guessed that she was now down to the level where the ballast would be stored and where any bilge water would accumulate. She knew that if there were any rats they would be there as well.

However, since she was near the bow of the vessel, the boards immediately beneath her were fairly dry. Dark and fearsome though the hiding place was, it was better than being hunted by Slobbit. Painstakingly she struggled with the hatch above her head and at last it dropped into place. In the darkness she could hear the waves lapping outside the hull and the occasional creak of the timbers. Her clothes were sopping wet and she was cold. But she had often been uncomfortable. Life had never treated her very kindly, so she curled herself up tightly into a self-warming ball and fell asleep.

She woke to the sounds of the vessel in motion. Her hiding place was no longer quiet. The rush of the bows through the water caused the waves to swish and bubble beneath the prow. Only the planking was between her and the sea. It was like hiding under a waterfall. From above her came the rhythmic sweep

and creak of the oars. It wasn't quite the same as a sailing vessel. The oars entered the water together and, with the stroke of the oarsmen, there was a perceptible surge forward, then a slight lull and another surge as the oars met the wavelets again.

People were singing, talking and laughing together. There were sounds of banging and voices cheerfully calling to each other. The ship seemed alive, swaying with the billows as she leaped forward. Sorrel pressed her body closer to the timbers, wedging herself up into the corner against one of the rib timbers. She was beginning to have second thoughts about having come on board. She was so very cold and wet and there seemed no hope of getting dry.

Suddenly she heard voices from directly above her. Two men were standing within inches of her hiding place and she could hear every word of their conversation.

'The Captain says it will all be over very soon now — after all these years of preparation.'

'Yes, it's great to be sailing at last. Just think of sharing in the triumph — the whole sea full of vessels like ours, sounding our trumpets, greeting the new kingdom.'

'I can hardly imagine what it will be like — to see that great fountain of life the Daylord talks about. I had a lump in my throat last night when the Cap'n was describing the lights, the colours and the glory.'

'Yes, sometimes when I listen to Melody or the Cap'n talking, I could think that they'd already seen it. They describe everything so well.'

'But the real thing will be better than all those descriptions.'

At that very moment, and without any warning at all, Sorrel let out an enormous sneeze. She had no idea that she was going to sneeze; the tickle took her completely by surprise.

'That solves that mystery' said the first man calmly. 'The Cap'n will be pleased. You wait here, I'll get him.'

She heard footsteps move away and held her breath. The voice of the remaining sailor came distinctly, she guessed he was now kneeling by the trapdoor.

'Now don't you worry yourself lass. It's going to be a lovely day. You'll be all right. We'll have you out of there in a jiffy.'

Tears began to run down Sorrel's cheeks, but she brushed them angrily away. Suddenly she heard a woman's voice — half angry, half joking.

'Men!' the voice exclaimed. 'Send for the Captain indeed! Whatever next? Now you go and peel potatoes. We'll see to this!'

'Let me give you a hand with the trapdoor' suggested the sailor apologetically.

'All right' was the reply. 'But then be off with you. The poor kid will be upset. It's cold and dark down there!'

At that Sorrel's chin snapped up. She didn't think of herself as a kid, let alone a poor kid. She didn't want pity. So as the first chink of light came down through the hatch it lit up two large indignant eyes.

'Come on up' said a voice and hands were reached down to help her. Two girls were smiling down at her.

One was about a year older than Sorrel and the other looked like an older sister — a girl in her early twenties.

The older girl's voice had a lilt that softened Sorrel at once.

'I'm Dawn' she said. 'You must have been terribly uncomfortable down there. It's quite safe you know. We guessed you were on board somewhere. We found your shoes on the beach.'

From Sorrel's point of view, the next few hours were sheer bliss. Dawn and Zoe took complete charge of her and made a great fuss of her. There were endless supplies of hot water, fragrant soaps, freshly heated towels and warm and flattering clothes. They did her hair, manicured her nails and gave her hot chocolate to drink. She was allocated a tiny cabin of her own, with a comfortable bunk and flowers and fruit.

'You're treating me like an invalid!' Sorrel exclaimed. 'It was only one sneeze; there was sawdust down there.'

'Never mind' said Zoe. 'Make the most of it. They don't fuss over me like this.'

Much later Sorrel was taken to meet the Captain and the crew. To get to the central cabin she had to pass along the deck where the rowers were labouring. She had been a little fearful of this, wondering whether there would be convicts or galley slaves and maybe a man with a whip urging them on.

But it was nothing like that at all. To her amazement girls were rowing alongside fellows. Everyone was working hard but none looked strained or forced in any way. They sang softly in time with the sweep of the oars and the craft seemed to skim over the blue waters. The sun was high in the sky now, and the red gold of the woodwork was splashed with patches of light and shade. The air was fresh, but pleasantly warm.

They passed through the main cabin and then across the deck to the aft cabin which belonged to the Captain. It was a bright and cheerful room in the stern of the vessel. It contained some furniture — some chairs and a table, but everything was functional. The beauty came from skilfully embroidered drapes and tapestries. Behind the Captain's table was a wide window looking out from the stern of the vessel over the wake. Sorrel could see the waves foaming white where the ship was swiftly gliding. The sun was sparkling on the crests of the waves. It was like looking down a golden highway.

Sorrel had already met the Captain at Dove Cottage. Aboard his own ship he seemed confident and cheerful. His complexion was sun tanned, he had a fine black beard and his eyes were deep blue. His handshake was warm and friendly.

'Welcome aboard Sorrel' he said. 'The Daylord has commissioned us to sail to Diamede. Hundreds of other ships will be going too. We must be there to greet the fountain of light which the old stories tell us about. We hope to arrive when the four carpenters sound their trumpets and to see the new kingdom and the royal family. What do you say? Would you like to see all these things and to come with us?'

Sorrel looked at him doubtfully.

'I find it a bit hard to believe' she explained. 'But since I was at Dove Cottage I've learned a lot and I think I'll get there in the end. But you'll have to be patient with me.' She swallowed hard and meeting his eyes admitted bravely,

'I stole Harmony's purse a long time ago and there was money in it.'

'Cheer up!' said the Captain. 'Harmony has her purse and all the money. In any case she would have helped you at the time if you'd asked. I think the Daylord hoped you'd ask, then you could have worked at Dove Cottage instead of Dunroamin. But never mind.' He turned and looked out over the foaming wake of the vessel. 'You know Sorrel, every single one of us has done things that were wrong. Perhaps we feel closer to one another because of that. Not one of us feels proud. But we're all very happy because we know that the Daylord has forgiven us. So when I said, "Welcome aboard" I really meant it.'

All the crew made Sorrel feel welcome. When she joined a group of people there were no unkind words, no reproachful glances, no whispering in corners and no awkward silences. Dawn and Zoe became her special friends. The only thing that irritated her was a little joke that they had between them. They would refer to themselves as her ladies in waiting and Sorrel found this difficult. In the afternoon there was a flare up.

'Stop it!'

Dawn and Zoe looked at Sorrel with surprise, their

faces distressed. Sorrel's cheeks were aflame and her eyes sultry with pent up fury. She scowled at them.

'Whatever's the matter, Sorrel?' asked Dawn.

Sorrel stamped her foot.

'You're all so ... so ... KIND!' she burst out. 'You keep treating me as though I were someone special. I can't bear it. I don't mind you feeding and clothing me. I'm grateful for that. But if only you'd let me be what I am.'

'What are you Sorrel?' asked Zoe cautiously.

'I'm a servant. That's what I am. A serving girl. I can cook, polish, make beds and light fires. I know my place. Treat me like that and I'll feel comfortable. Give me orders and I'll do what you say. I'll earn my passage. I'll row if you let me. I can row you know.'

Dawn was smiling at her.

'Oh Sorrel!' she said gently 'You still don't under-stand about the Daylord, do you?'

Sorrel stared at her without replying and Dawn went on.

'We believe in the Daylord and what he did in another place and another time. Because we trust in him, he has said that we are all princes and prin-cesses. We are all his servants, but we are all royalty as well. He says that we're not to think of ourselves as mere servants, but to be part of his family. It's all in the old stories — and we believe them.'

'I think we should show her' said Zoe.

'Yes' agreed Dawn. 'Let's take her down to the cabin.'

They went into the big room in the middle of the ship. The sun was now streaming through portholes.

Zoe disappeared for a moment and came back struggling through the doorway with a huge shield almost as big as herself.

'Roll it along the floor.' suggested Dawn. 'It's almost too big for you. You ought to have brought one your own size.'

'I wanted a big one' replied Zoe. 'I want Sorrel to get a good view.'

Sorrel recognised the shield as one of those she had seen hanging over the side of the vessel. Seen close up, it was enormous. She gasped as she realised that it was fashioned out of beautifully ornamented gold.

'Now' said Dawn encouragingly 'stand in front of that and look at yourself.'

The mirror before her dazzled and flashed like the sun itself and it was almost too difficult to see her reflection.

Sorrel had to move sideways to get the angle of the light right as the shield flung back the rays of the sun from a myriad of planed surfaces. The shield was all mirrors and in each one she saw a reflection. But what she saw was a princess with a circlet of diamonds on her head. She was wearing a robe of white satin or silk and it was delicately embroidered like a wedding dress. A rich necklace glittered at her neck and there was a bracelet on her arm. A purple sash swept from her shoulder to her waist and her high heeled shoes were encrusted with diamonds. Sorrel staggered for a moment and then turned away angrily.

'That isn't me!' she flared again 'You're playing some kind of trick.'

But the girls had crept away, closing the door behind them. She was completely alone. Hardly daring to look, Sorrel edged forward and stood again in the light reflected from the great shield. She moved her hand and so did the figure in the shield. She turned and glanced over her shoulder. It certainly did seem to be her reflection. Yet, when she looked down at her own clothes, they were quite ordinary — pretty enough, but certainly not regal. She shrugged her shoulders and the figure also shrugged. She put out her tongue and went cross eyed. The royal princess did the same. The reflection looked so ridiculous that she laughed, and the reflection laughed too — showing white teeth, dimples and dancing eyes. Suddenly Sorrel found herself laughing and crying all at once. Gradually she was beginning to understand about the Daylord and the stories.

Later Dawn returned on her own and sat with her arm round Sorrel for a while. As she talked in her lilting voice about the Daylord, Sorrel felt comforted and cheered in a way that she had never known before.

CHAPTER 21
TO DIAMEDE

*D*riftwood sailed on through the morning and early afternoon. On his way he passed a small cove with a few houses and three fishermen's boats lying at anchor. He took his dinghy into the cove and went ashore to stretch his legs and to find what provisions he could.

There was only one village store but he was able to buy some basic necessities. He was afraid that someone might recognise him, although the village was so remote that there was little risk of that. He put to sea again as soon as he could. It was late afternoon before he found another small sandy cove where there were no houses at all. A brook tumbled down the cliff face and flowed out into the sea — so he was able to get water to drink.

He gathered together some dry wood from above the tide mark and also pulled up some dry grasses and dead wood for some kindling. Soon the fire was blaz-

ing merrily and blue smoke was curling into the air. The wood crackled and blazed and Driftwood was kept busy feeding the fire. He enjoyed the smell of the woodsmoke mingled with the briny tang of the sea.

He cooked sausages stuck on the end of twigs and broke up hunks of fresh bread. Having feasted himself, he lay contentedly by the fire. There was no road or pathway near the bay so he was safer than at any time until now. After a while he fell asleep. Towards the middle of the night he woke and built up the fire. At about 3 a.m. he awoke again. This time there was a sea mist and he was bitterly cold. He fed the fire from the pile of wood that he had collected earlier and it was soon blazing cheerily again. He drowsed in its heat till dawn broke. Then he rigged the dinghy and set sail again. The wind was still favourable and most of that day he sailed with the castle of Diamede clearly visible on the distant horizon.

By afternoon he was close enough to fear that he might be observed, so he went ashore and hid the boat. He still had no clear plan of how to get into the castle, or of what he would do to rescue Strug and Stumble when he arrived. However, whenever he held the pearl in his hand, the tug was strong and insistent. He was meant to go to Diamede, somehow he sensed that this was his destiny.

He knew that he would have to leave the dinghy behind. There was a strong current around the headland on which Diamede was built. The tides raced and the seas were never still. Great breakers rolled and crashed against the shore. The rest of his journey would need to be made on foot. He put his provisions into the canvas bag which was usually used to stow away the sails, and slinging this over his shoulder, he followed a sheep track which ran close to the water's edge.

He noted that the tide was coming in — although the boat was safely stowed away well above high water mark. No harm would come to it. He headed on, reasonably confident that no one would be watching a path so close to the water and one which was well hidden from any Dreirds in the garrison of Diamede.

After some while he heard a new tone in the roar of the surf and came to a place where the sea surged through a narrow inlet. Looking inland he could see in the distance the dark entrance to a cavern with a cliff opposite it which was pitted with caves and overhanging cliffs. It would be difficult to pick his way across the boulders round the shore line. But there were still some rocks and boulders here and there above the water line at the mouth of the inlet. He felt sure that he could safely use the rocks as stepping stones and find his way across. He set out confidently.

Before long he realised that he was taking something of a risk. Some of the boulders were dry, but others were already awash with the incoming tide and were also slimy with seaweed. There was a risk that the force of the water might sweep him off them. He half considered turning back — but that would mean lost time and he wasn't sure whether he could get past the inlet without spending dangerous hours clambering on the cliffs. So he pressed on, thankful that the tide was no higher.

As he neared the other shore, he had to venture a soaking. The last boulder between him and the safety of the other shore was well submerged with waves foaming over it. He stood a few moments waiting. Some of the waves were larger than others and after a few big ones had swept by and there seemed to be a lull, he took a risk, stumbled and got a wetting, but he managed to scramble to safety without any real danger. Stopping for a moment, he gazed back to trace that path that he had taken among the smooth boulders and foaming waves.

When Sorrel came on board, the Captain had a look-out posted to try to spot Driftwood's dinghy and to scan the shoreline for any clue as to his whereabouts. Towards late afternoon there came a shout.

'Dinghy above high water mark, Cap'n.'

The Captain ran up on deck and Sorrel joined him with Dawn and Zoe. Driftwood's dinghy was well hidden from anybody walking on the land. Viewed from the sea it could be spotted but only with difficulty. The Captain congratulated the look-out on his sharp eyes.

'Is that Driftwood's dinghy Sorrel?' he asked as he passed her his brass telescope.

Sorrel had some difficulty adjusting the telescope and training it on the distant shoreline. But once the dinghy came into focus she was in no doubt at all.

'He's hidden it just like we did before' she said. 'He must be somewhere near at hand. Please let me go ashore and look for him.'

'What do you think, Dawn?' asked the Captain. She nodded.

'We were expecting this. Zoe and I were thinking about the Daylord today and we both sensed that Sorrel would have to go to look for Driftwood — and go alone.'

'Alone!' exclaimed the Captain. 'I don't like the idea of that at all.'

'No more do we' Dawn agreed. 'Do you think we've got it wrong? I know we do make mistakes sometimes. What do you think?'

'I think I'd like to take a search party ashore' said the Captain, turning to the look-out. 'Prepare the pinnace! You girls wait here and I'll consult with the chief officers.'

The crew rested on their oars and the pinnace was lowered into the water — by which time the Captain had returned.

'It's to be just as Sorrel has asked' he said shaking his head gravely. 'We find the Daylord quite definite about that. So we must do what he wants'

'You don't sound very happy about it' said Zoe cheekily.

The Captain still looked serious.

'When you set out on a voyage you know there will be storms as well as sunshine' he remarked. 'Are you ready for that Sorrel?'

'Of course she is!' retorted Zoe. 'Girls are good at facing up to things — just as good as boys you know!' Dawn put out a hand and touched Zoe on the forearm.

'I wish you'd let me go with Sorrel' she said. 'I know I ought not to be anxious about anything the Daylord says, but I can't help feeling afraid for her.'

'The sooner I get going, the sooner Driftwood and I will be back' said Sorrel. 'Let's not waste time talking.'

Eight strong oarsmen in jerseys manned the pinnace and they were soon close to the shore. Strong arms helped her up onto the beach.

'If I am not back in two hours, you must go without me' said Sorrel.

On board ship the Captain stood with the white bird perched on his shoulder. It seemed amazingly tame and was gently rubbing the Captain's ear with its beak. After a few moments the Captain took the bird in his hands.

'You'll let me know how she gets on?' he whispered and it almost seemed to nod in reply. Then holding up both hands he released it. The bird flew skywards, circling the boat. Its wings seemed very large for a pigeon and its lazy wing beat was more like that of a soaring eagle. Using thermal currents it was soon so high in the sky that it was no more than a distant speck. None of the crew were surprised by this. Long ago they had discovered that Melody's birds —like the carpenter's horses — had their real home in another place and another time.

It was warmer on shore than on the water. Insects were buzzing and there was the heavy scent of ferns. Sorrel hunted this way and that, but guessed that Driftwood would probably be travelling in the direction of Diamede. So she set out along the shoreline until she began to hear a changed note in the roar of the surf.

It was a deeper and more thundering sound and as she rounded a corner of rocks she came to an inlet where waves were rushing and foaming up the channel towards a distant cave. The opposite shore was honeycombed with caverns and it was as she looked towards the foreshore in front of the caves that she spotted Driftwood's distant figure. Eagerly she began to wave and shout, but he couldn't hear her. She couldn't reach him because the incoming tide had covered the boulders and the tidal flow was now a fierce current. No swimmer could ever hope to get across.

Sorrel was in agony with Driftwood so near to her, yet out of reach and clearly unable to hear her words or understand her signals. From her vantage point she could see something that he had entirely missed. Driftwood was standing on a narrow strip of hard sand on the other side of the white water, and about seven metres above him was a narrow ledge. From then on the cliff rose sheer, but here and there it was dotted with pits and caves.

Sorrel's first thought, like Driftwood's, had been whether it was possible to clamber along the sides of the inlet. But like him she realised that it would be an arduous if not impossible task to clamber among bare rock faces, cliffs and overhanging crags. As she searched for a way, her eyes rested on the cliff immediately above Driftwood. Something was moving in the entrance to the nearest cave. Even at that distance she could recognise the ungainly form of Slobbit. He'd emerged stealthily from the cave entrance with a large fisherman's net in his arms. He was now crouched on the ledge above Driftwood's head and was preparing to drop the net over him.

Just at that moment Driftwood caught sight of Sorrel on the other side of the inlet. She shouted frantically and gesticulated, but the wind carried her voice away and Driftwood clearly couldn't understand what she was shouting or waving about.Slowly, terrifyingly the drama was acted out before her eyes and she was helpless to do anything about it.

Patiently Slobbit waited with his net, peering down through the meshes, watching every move Driftwood made. All Driftwood's attention was focussed on Sorrel; he was totally oblivious of the threatening figure poised above him. In any case the roar of the water would have covered any scrabbling sounds that Slobbit might have made. Suddenly and deftly Slobbit flipped his net out and over the ledge. Down it came trapping Driftwood neatly in the middle.

Sorrel saw Slobbit leap down. With all the speed of a spider spinning webs round its victim, he gathered up the folds of the net till Driftwood was cocooned inside it. There was nothing Sorrel could do. Of course Slobbit couldn't reach her. She was safe enough. But Driftwood was now a helpless captive. Slobbit dragged him along the sand towards the lower end of the cliff and then slung him over his powerful shoulders as a miller might carry a sack of flour. Slobbit took his burden up to the cave entrance and disappeared into the rocky tunnel. Sorrel was alone again.

Slobbit didn't take Driftwood far. The cave was in fact the entrance to a tunnel which led from Diamede castle. A badly rusted iron gate stood half open. Slobbit carried Driftwood through it, pulled it shut and padlocked it. Then he disentangled Driftwood from the net and put a noose round his neck. For a moment Driftwood thought that he was to be hanged there and then, but Slobbit simply jerked on the rope and tugged him towards a flight of stone steps that led upwards into the clammy darkness.

'Up' Slobbit commanded. 'You see Fowler first. Then he'll be pleased with Slobbit.'

So Driftwood, easing the rope around his neck with one hand, climbed up the steps as quickly as he could with Slobbit following behind. He guided himself by means of an iron railing, but fit as he was, he soon began to lose his breath. He guessed that they were making their way towards the pinnacle of rock on which Diamede itself was built. Eventually the air seemed to smell cold, fresh and salty, and before long he could see a circle of light above him. He stood blinking in the fresh air. Before him a rope walkway led across to the actual pinnacle.

Glancing up he could see the underside of the drawbridge far above him. That was used for horses, carriages and carts bringing provisions. The precarious rope walkway was simply some kind of servants' entrance, giving access to the beach below. If there was any kind of siege, the walkway could be slashed away in a moment from either side, leaving the citadel impregnable.

Driftwood now understood why Slobbit had not bound his hands. He needed them to cling on as he

struggled across the narrow rope bridge. The wind caught at him and the slender construction swayed. But it was safe and before long they had reached the entrance to the pinnacle. Above them was the splendour of the castle. But this was clearly a gateway used by menials. The main entrance far above them was splendid and imposing.

There was nothing grand about this way in. The many tunnels were like mine workings, and although the occasional candle lantern guttered from a wrought iron socket, the atmosphere spoke of dungeons and dreary passageways. Driftwood knew that here would be the solitary cells where prisoners were left in wretched captivity until they were forgotten by the whole world. Here too would be torture chambers and all kinds of horrors. He knew that humanly speaking he stood little chance of escape, but he still had the feeling that he was meant to come and that gave him some courage in a situation full of despair.

Slobbit shoved him down various flights of stairs. Clearly he wasn't going to see the splendid royal apartments. He was a prisoner and no doubt about it.

'I haven't done you any harm, Slobbit' he pleaded. 'Why are you treating me like this?'

'Fowler wants Driftwood. He'll give Slobbit present.'

Slobbit pushed Driftwood again, and he nearly lost his footing on the stairs. Eventually they came to a kind of guard chamber deep in the heart of Diamede. Some Dreird guards were sitting staring vacantly in front of them. Unlike ordinary human beings they needed no pastime to occupy them. When left without orders, they simply sat staring blankly. However they took Driftwood readily enough, and manhandled him none too gently into an inner cave with an iron door that clanged shut. For the present he was entombed with no possibility of escape.

CHAPTER 22
THE CASTLE

*S*trug and Stumbles' cart creaked and rattled over the cobblestones as they entered the city of Diamede. High in the distance stood the castle. It was separated from the rest of the city and was built upon a solitary pinnacle of rock at the extreme end of the island. It could be reached only by means of a great drawbridge which, when raised, rendered the fortress completely inaccessible from the mainland.

Far below, angry and tumultuous seas surged around the base of the pinnacle and between it and the cliff of the mainland. No ship could pass through the fierce race of wild waters and no swimmer could survive the battering of those combing breakers.

The city itself was pleasant enough. It had broad streets, several parks and gracious houses. It lacked the surface gaiety of Heartsease, but it had the feel of a capital city. The inhabitants were ordinary, most of them concerned about their own affairs. They were

wary of talking politics, because everyone knew that Dreird spies were among them. Apart from that, life went on as usual.

Strug and Stumble found lodgings in an old Inn. Stumble fed the horse and rubbed him down; Strug went to bed early. Of the two men, Stumble was less affected by the Dreadwater than Strug, but both of them were in the grip of terrible illness.

Next morning they drove their cart towards the great drawbridge. A Dreird official demanded that they complete forms in triplicate before they were allowed to enter. It was mid morning before the cart was permitted to go over the bridge and under the portcullis.

Once inside the castle precincts Dreirds surrounded them. The stone carving was accepted and carried inside the main hall of the castle. A Dreird led the horse and cart away to the stables. After another wearisome wait, some Dreird guards in smart uniform appeared and Strug and Stumble were led towards the main entrance of the castle.

First they climbed a great flight of steps, then they went on through tall columns, roofs arched high above and inner courtyards. They passed neatly tended lawns, statues and fountains. All the time they were climbing towards the magnificent central structure of the castle. Great doors stood open, doors profusely ornamented with gold and splendid carvings.

Now the pavement beneath their feet displayed a brilliant highly polished marble pattern. They passed through a great armoury and then into the audience chamber itself. As they entered the stateroom, a great bell tolled from the tower above them, its sonorous echoes reverberating through the halls and corridors and out into the courtyards beyond.

King Threld sat in royal state upon a splendid throne, behind him a representation of the rising sun which was made of what appeared to be solid gold. Above that, the great wall was draped with scarlet velvet hangings. The throne was of gold, richly inlaid with gems. It had six steps by which it could be approached and on each step stood the image of a great cat carved of ebony. King Threld himself, robed in splendour, sat holding a royal sceptre in his lap. His crown sparkled and flashed in the flickering flames of great torches that blazed in a long avenue down the length of the hall.

The entire floor of the hall was an amazing mosaic of different woods. The centre was a great circle divided into segments, but the whole surface was an intricate mixture of geometric designs. The woods were from many different kinds of tree: walnut, oak, mahogany, and other more exotic woods to give life and colour.

Strug and Stumble bowed low at the door and then began their approach towards the throne. Strug was more hunched than ever and needed Stumble to support him. Stumble was still lean and wiry. He had an anxious face, toil worn hands and haggard features. They hobbled forward together. The surface of the wood was highly polished. They could see their reflections in it, but it was very difficult to walk on — almost like stepping on ice. Slowly they made their way to the wooden circle before the throne where they were to present their petition to the great king.

At long last they arrived at a thick silken rope suspended from golden posts which prevented them going further. Still King Threld sat silent on his throne. Stumble cleared his throat and glanced upwards towards the royal countenance. Only then did his old eyes perceive the truth. He was gazing at a quartz figure. King Threld was a lifeless statue. At his right hand stood the beautiful Queen. A glass raised to her lips as if in the act of drinking a toast, her eyes sparkling, but sightless.

The two stone horses that Strug and Stumble had brought with them had been set down close to the steps leading to the throne. And now, echoing round the great hall was a voice. Presumably Fowler was standing somewhere in the shadows, but he could not be seen.

'Welcome to Diamede my old friends. You see King Threld in all his majesty, but you appreciate that your plea for help will fall on deaf ears. There are two matters, the second shall be first. You should have submitted to my will and remained at Black Tor. However I am pleased with the carving that you have brought to Diamede. It graces this hall. King Threld and I are happy to receive it.

The first matter comes second. You will remain in this hall. The Dreirds have orders that you shall not leave the castle but will stay here in great uncertainty. This hall is known as the Place of Disquiet. You have paced across its floor, not knowing that it is an intricate pattern of trapdoors. Any one of these doors may suddenly open beneath your feet. No place where you choose to stand is safe ground. Even were you so bold as to clamber upon the image itself, there is no security — not even on the throne.

Beneath the floor are the deep caverns of Diamede. There are galleries of quartz and stalactites and stalagmites of exquisite beauty. But in the centre, and in great depths below, lies the pool of Dreadwater which has collected over aeons of time. You will stay here upon the floor of the Place of Disquiet. Sooner or later I shall pull a lever and your anxiety will be replaced by terror as you plummet into the pool which turns everything it touches into quartz. It may be today; it may be tomorrow. You will be given food and drink as befits royal visitors, but at last when the mood seizes me, I shall dispose of you forever.'

Strug tottered on his feet, but raised his head with an effort to gaze into his loved brother's face.

'Always talking that there Fowler. Aye. Always talk, talk, talk — and no manners at all. We're in for a long wait my brother. Aye. But old Black Tor has taught us how to wait.'

CHAPTER 23
ROYAL CARPENTERS

*S*orrel was desperate. Slobbit had dragged Driftwood off, and there was nothing she could do to prevent it. Driftwood must be somewhere inside the fortress of Diamede — probably in a dungeon. Perhaps they would torture him. The situation was dreadful. She felt so helpless and alone. Running as fast as she could, she turned to make her way back to the pinnace, but the incoming tide forced her to make a detour.

She came across a track leading upwards and a carved signpost pointing out a path to Diamede Clock Tower. There were no reward notices posted about Sorrel, so she wasn't in the same danger as Driftwood had been. Slobbit was the only enemy she needed to fear and she knew where he was. It seemed to Sorrel that the best hope was to try to find Strug and Stumble in Diamede. Perhaps together they could persuade King Threld to have mercy and to force Fowler to

release Driftwood. Sorrel would willingly make apple pies for Slobbit for the rest of her life if it meant that she could bribe him to let Driftwood go. It seemed pointless to go back to the ship. She would do better to press on.

It was a stiff upwards climb, but here and there logs had been used to make steps and to prevent erosion. In very steep places there were handrails to help and the path was clearly marked. It led to the top of the cliffs and onto the main road leading to the city of Diamede which ran well away from the caves that honeycombed the hillside below. Once on level ground Sorrel set a steady pace. She would run for about twenty paces, then walk for twenty paces, then run again. She was making good speed and getting close to the city gates when she heard the brisk trot of horses behind her.

Looking over her shoulder, she saw an open Landau. The carriage was drawn by fine horses. Two Dreirds on horseback were ahead and four more rode behind. A Dreird was driving the Landau, but lolling back on the cushions was the stout sandy haired figure of Glummit. Sorrel recognised him immediately from Driftwood's description but she had no way of knowing if Glummit would recognise her. She never realised that she had been spotted by the Dreirds when she left Dove Cottage. On that occasion Glummit had let her go because he hadn't seen any use for her.

Sorrel's capture was the easiest thing in the world as far as Glummit was concerned. As the Landau drew alongside Sorrel, he spoke to the coachman, who brought it to a halt.

"'ello my beauty!' he leered down at Sorrel.

'Just the gal to make my little cup o' 'appiness overflow! Look lively now and jump aboard, else my friend 'ere'll tickle you with 'is 'orsewhip. 'ere give us your 'and.' There was nothing for it. Sorrel allowed herself to be helped up into the Landau. She rode into Diamede sitting opposite Glummit who shot her sideways glances, sucking his moustache from time to time, and muttering to himself.

Glummit had not overlooked the fact that Fowler had intended to turn him to quartz by leaving a bottle of Dreadwater as a present. But he was still confident that he could persuade Fowler that he would make a more useful conspirator than Slobbit. He was not sure whether Fowler had really expected to trap him with the bottle. He suspected that the episode might well have been a sort of entrance examination, a simple test to see how cunning Glummit was. That's how Fowler's mind would work. If Glummit was no use, he would drink the Dreadwater. If he was smart, then he would use the Dreadwater against Slobbit. And Glummit had been smart. In fact he had been more cunning than Fowler because he had bottled a supply of Dreadwater in one of Fowler's own decanters. He came out in a cold sweat every time he thought of the dangers. But long experience in handling liquor at the Tipsy Goose had been a help to him and he had been able to pour and store a small quantity without a drop touching him.

Carrying the decanter he felt much like a soldier carrying a live grenade. The risk was enormous, but if he was turned to quartz, so would everyone else around him. He reasoned that even if Fowler was completely covered with barrier cream, he would still be unable to protect his eyes. If Fowler attacked Glummit, he would splash Dreadwater in Fowler's face. Yes, Glummit had plenty to think about as he approached Diamede and when Glummit was thinking he also muttered aloud. But he took good care that Sorrel heard nothing of what he was saying under his breath.

'Power — that's what it is, Glummit me ol' pal. Power an' wealth. You can 'ave wotever you want, so long as you play your cards right. Worm your way into ol' Fowlers 'eart. That's if 'es got a 'eart. It'll take a lot o' wormin' an' that's for sure. Still 'e does need me. Even if 'e don't know it yet. 'Es got to 'ave someone to do 'is dirty work for 'im and I'm the man ain't I? Then once I've wormed away and got the secret of the barrier cream, then it's curtains for Fowler!' Glummit glanced slyly at the girl opposite.

'Tryin' not to look scared ain't she. She is scared though, an' 'as reason to be. Fowler won't arf be glad to see 'er. 'ostage, that's wot she is. Driftwood 'ud do anythin' to see 'er safely out o' it.'

So it was that Glummit's search party cantered briskly towards Diamede, reported to the Dreirds by the Drawbridge and received permission to enter the castle for an audience with Fowler. Glummit was careful that the Dreirds informed Fowler that he was bringing in Sorrel for questioning. Clutching her arm tightly, he dragged her struggling into the maze of tunnels, stairways and caverns that lay below the state apartments of Diamede.

Strug and Stumble were brave old men, but they knew that there was no conflict between prayer and courage. Because they only knew one prayer, they began to mutter it again and again.

'Oh thou the unknown who givest light, give more light.'

There was a commotion outside the great doors.

''ere don't you fight with me, yer young vixen. I'll beat the livin' daylights out of you, that's what I'll do. Your my passport to Mr Fowler, that's what you are. Hold still won't yer.'

It was Glummit dragging a struggling Sorrel along by one arm. She was trying to hold back, but once her feet were on the polished floor of the hall there was nothing more she could do but allow herself to be dragged across it. A Dreird with impassive face was leading the way and two more Dreirds followed behind. Sorrel had never met Driftwood's guardians and she didn't recognise the two frail old men hunched in prayer near the throne of the King. But she did hear their murmured prayer.

'Oh thou the unknown who givest light, give more light.'

Even in her own dreadful need, the prayer the old men were muttering seemed so sad to her. Things had been so different with the happy crew aboard the ship.

'Don't you know' she cried eagerly as Glummit dragged her past them 'you're praying it wrong. It's not the unknown ... it's the Daylord who gives light.'

227

'Stop blabbing an' come along' snapped Glummit. 'We're goin' to see Mr Fowler, you an' me, and you ain't goin' to enjoy it , I tell yer.'

The Dreird opened a door and Glummit pushed Sorrel towards a flight of steps. His voice was still running on as the door closed and was locked behind him.

Left alone in the great hall, Strug and Stumble looked at one another. Stumble scratched his ear thoughtfully.

'If only I could remember' he said sadly.

'Try saying what she said' suggested Strug. 'It can't do any harm. The words might come back to us.'

So bowing their heads they started again. 'Oh thou the Daylord who givest light ...'

Far in the distance, thunder rumbled as if in immediate answer to their words. No sooner had it died away than it was followed by another louder crash that reverberated round the hall. Although the Palace was locked and the windows sealed, a cool breeze sighed through the corridors.

'There's the beginning of a storm up at Black Tor brother' said Stumble.

'Aye. Do you remember the great storm?' replied Strug.

'The night we found young Driftwood? Aye I remember. That was meant to be brother, that was meant to be.'

'Aye, but how did we come to be there — on Black Tor I mean?'

'My horse fell' said Stumble.

'Your horse, yes I remember now. It lost a shoe that night, struck against the stone of the Tor it did. I'd forgotten you had a horse. Now what was its name?'

Stumble rubbed his forehead fretfully. 'My poor old brain' he cried. 'Let me think. 'Ply something or other it was. Plywood — no — Pliable — no. If only I could think.' He paused.

'Pleiades' said Strug. I remember it clearly. Funny name for a workman's horse. Fancy calling him "Pleiades"!'

'You're a fine one to talk, brother. You called yours "Conquest."'

If their backs hadn't been turned to the two carved stone horses, they would have seen the ears prick and the eyes begin to roll. Subtle fires were running over mane and tails.

'Pleiades and Conquest' said Stumble, half to himself, but he was answered by a triumphant neighing and clattering of hooves. Silver harnesses rattled and two magnificent stallions began nuzzling at their masters' elbows. Strug straightened his back and seemed to grow stronger and taller. Stumble felt a young man's strength surging back into his limbs.

'It must have been the Old Tor that stole our memories brother. I know now who we are.'

'Aye' cried Strug. 'Not miners and quarrymen, nor hewers of stone. We're royal carpenters and always have been.'

'We even forgot our own names' agreed Stumble. 'Your real name is Strong, not Strug, and mine is Storm, not Stumble. At last we're remembering. The

Daylord gives light, my brother. The Daylord gives light.'

As they swung up into their saddles, they were transformed. They sat firm and erect on their steeds, clothed as warrior lords of the great King. In their hands they carried golden trumpets of victory.

'Do we sound the call, brother?' asked Stumble eagerly.

'Nay my old friend. Remember — only when the Daylord says, "Now." But at least we can put the Dreirds to flight and let down the drawbridge. 'Tis four carpenters to fray, remember? And Calm and Chuckle are waiting outside.'

CHAPTER 24
THE CAVERN

*T*he cavern of Dreadwater lay deep in the heart of the pinnacle of rock on which the castle of Diamede had been built. When Fowler first discovered this cavern he had been accompanied only by a guard dog.

Once he had discovered how diluted Dreadwater could enslave people as Dreirds, he had a plentiful supply of cheap labour with which to improve the cavern. Ventilation shafts had been provided and Dreirds, labouring in patient slavery, worked pumps to keep the air supply fresh. Similarly torches were replenished at all hours of the day and night. Fowler had even had a lift installed for his use. It was driven by a steam engine located in a shed high above them.

Glummit and Sorrel weren't allowed to use Fowler's lift so Dreirds conducted them along corridors, down stairways, through stone galleries and past dungeons and closed doorways. Lower and lower they

went, till at last they stood at the top of a flight of steps leading down into the cavern of Dreadwater.

It was a sight of unimagineable beauty. Stalactites and stalagmites had formed everywhere. Some seemed to be of crystal, but most were of beautifully coloured and translucent quartz. There were numerous caves and grottoes at different levels within the walls of the main cavern. At the centre of the cavern and in its lowest depths there lay a crater whose steeply sloping sides were mostly glittering quartz as smooth as glass. Here and there were streaks of granules, almost like coarse sugar in appearance.

At the bottom of the crater was a pool of dark water. It seemed to be very deep, and totally stagnant. There were Dreirds moving about in the cavern. Fowler himself had his private entrance and this led directly to a throne high in the wall like a box at the theatre. From here he could watch everything and see his commands carried out without any risk of personal attack.

As Glummit and Sorrel were motioned to stand on a raised quartz platform in front of the throne, Sorrel could see that Fowler had lavished money on making his seat of power awe inspiring and intimidating. The basic design imitated the fan of a peacock's tail. Every kind of precious jewel had been used, and the richest silken fabrics. The actual throne was solid gold, and the canopy above sparkled with gems and gold filigree work. Mirrors were used to reflect light in such a way that it was very difficult to look at Fowler without being dazzled by the flashing lights. No king ever sat upon a more extravagantly designed throne. It was awesome and magnificent.

Glummit was clutching tightly to Sorrel's arm and she could feel him trembling. She realised that he was almost as afraid as she was, though for very different reasons.

'Two matters' said Fowler. His voice echoed around the cavern, his throne had been so situated that the whole cave magnified the sound of his speech.

'The second shall be first: you are welcome here. The first is that you, Sorrel, will never leave this place alive.'

'Just as you say, Mr Fowler sir' said Glummit. 'A right trouble she 'as been an' no mistake. So I guess it's alright if we speak freely like ain't it? Since she ain't goin' to tell on us like?'

Fowler inclined his head, and Glummit went on, becoming bolder as he warmed to his theme.

'You an' I can do business, Mr Fowler sir. As you see I've brought the girl 'ere. Now I ain't askin' for mercy, nor claimin' that you owe me anythin' neither. What I am sayin' is 'ow useful I can be to you. Just think Mr Fowler sir, a man with your interests at 'eart. You an' I understand one another sir, if I may make so bold. That's why when I saw that there bottle you left for me, I didn't get cross and I didn't drink it neither. I used it. Just like you would have done in my shoes.'

Fowler was silent a moment and then replied with dignity. 'Two matters, the second shall be first. The second is that I will employ you as you suggest upon one condition. The first is that to earn employment you must dispose of Sorrel in a way that will entertain me. That is the condition. The solution is within this cavern and you have ten minutes before I return. I trust to be amused.'

'Grab 'old o' the girl!' snapped Glummit to a Dreird. 'I must 'ave a quick look round and suss out this place.'

Sorrel felt a shiver of fear. The Dreird's face was bored and implacable. She could see the faint green of his breath as they stood in the shadows of the cave. Glummit was bustling around almost like someone planning a party. He was rubbing his hands and nodding to himself as he explored caverns and ledges, glanced up to the ceiling and peered round stalactites. She could hear his feet pattering here, there, everywhere.

'Where's Driftwood?' she asked herself. 'Has he been turned to quartz already? Are they torturing him somewhere?'

Suddenly a door clanged in the distance and she heard footsteps coming.

'Fowler pleased with Slobbit.' There was no mistaking the voice. Driftwood was in the grip of two powerful Dreirds, and Slobbit was ambling behind. Clearly he had not been told about Sorrel's capture for at the first sight of Sorrel, Slobbit let out a great roar of anger. Here was the wretch who had tried to poison him. He rushed straight at her, six fingered hands outstretched. But Glummit was too quick for him.

'Get 'im, Dreirds' he shouted. Six burly guards leaped upon Slobbit to restrain him. It was all that they could do to hold him, but it gave Sorrel the moment she wanted.

'Slobbit, it was Herbert not me. Hazy told him to poison you. But it was all Glummit's idea.'

Slobbit's goggle eyes swung round towards Glummit. Stupid though he was, he had never trusted Glummit, except when he had been drunk. Sorrel had been kind to him and given him apple pie. Glummit had more reason to get rid of him. It made a lot of sense to him.

With a great roar of anger he shook himself, spreading his arms in rage. The six great Dreirds were flung in all directions. In towering vengeance he advanced upon Glummit, but even as he stooped to grab his victim, Glummit quick as a flash whipped a sparkling bottle from behind his back and splashed liquid in Slobbit's eyes. It was over in a moment. The great barrel chested figure stood transfixed — a block of quartz. With infinite care Glummit placed the decanter upon the quartz floor. A sardonic hiss of laughter ran round the galleries of the cavern.

'So you have begun to pass the test. You are quick witted and well prepared.'

It was Fowler. He had only pretended to leave the cavern. All he had done was to walk down to the level where Sorrel and Driftwood were now standing.

'You see that I have taken the precaution of protecting my eyes' he said. 'However you need not fear me, Glummit. You prove to be cunning, and that is useful to me. ' Fowler paced round, staring at Driftwood, then at Sorrel. Finally he returned to face Glummit.

'Now,' he demanded 'what entertainment have you planned for me?'

Glummit had the manner of someone faced with an examination paper that pleased him.

'Well, now' he began 'before we comes to the question 'ow, first of all we 'as to consider the why.' He licked his moustache and glanced at the nearest stalactite, then he went on. 'An' there's also the question "who". Now I don't think Driftwood knows that, an' I don't think Sorrel does neither, but I do. An' why do I know it? Because of that lovely picture what 'angs over me bed at the Tipsy Goose.

'King Threld is quartz. His dear lady, very pretty and friendly like, is quartz. But their lovely little baby daughter what was born to them about the time Mr Fowler discovered the Dreadwater, she ain't quartz — yet. An' why not you ask? Because that same Mr Fowler needed somethin' to amuse 'isself. So what does 'e do, but give the baby to an old lady to nurse for 'im. Oh you 'as a right sense of 'umour you 'ave, Mr Fowler sir. You wanted to see that pretty little princess grow up and make a right mess of 'erself. You wanted 'er to gamble, an' steal, an' live like a criminal. You wanted 'er to be a serving wench, half starved and all thin and scraggy. An' it 'appened — just as you wanted, didn't it, Mr Fowler sir? And you was down at Threld Manor most of the time, watchin' an' gettin' all the news and keepin' it all to yourself!'

Driftwood, red faced with anger, struggled fiercely with the implacable guards who held him, but their grip was like iron.

'So that's it, Miss Sorrel' said Glummit 'Or Princess Sorrel p'raps I should say' he sucked his moustache. 'Now kind Mr Fowler 'ere as set me a little test. I 'ave to get rid of you in a way that will amuse 'im, see. An' 'ave I found such a way you ask?' Glummit glanced for a moment at her face and then his gaze shot away and fastened on the foot of a Dreird. 'Yes I 'ave. The first part of it of course, is that you 'ave to know who you really are. So I've just told you. The second part is that you need to 'ave time to get over bein' brave. Because it ain't goin' to amuse Mr Fowler if you just gets turned to quartz — not with you keepin' your chin up and lookin' all brave and good like you do at the moment. I guessed that Mr Fowler would 'ave somethin' already lined up for you, so I 'ad a look round an' you know what Sorrel? I've found it.'

'Bring her over here' he ordered the Dreirds. Sorrel was led to a kind of cage or cave let into the wall of the cavern. It was completely bare of any furnishings and there were iron bars across the entrance with a door through which Sorrel was pushed. She was standing inside a large prison cell. Glummit grinned at her cheerfully through the bars.

'Very interestin' idea' he chatted. 'One of Mr Fowler's best. Dreadwater drips through the ceiling you see. Not much, not often, a drip 'ere, a drip there. It's all quite slow an' natural. Nothin' that wasn't 'ere to begin with, except the iron bars of course. Now Sorrel you 'ave a problem...an' when you start thinkin' about it, you may get a little bit anxious an' 'ysterical like I wouldn't wonder. You see the drip can fall anywhere.

Maybe in front of you. Maybe behind you, one side or the other. It might fall on top of you, an' if it do, then you're done for. Trouble is, you don't know where the drip is goin' to fall, an' neither do I. You don't know when it's goin' to fall neither. An' when one misses you, the next one might get you. You can stan' still, or you can jump about. You can look at the roof and try an' spot it, or you can shut your eyes an' scream your 'ead off. Nighty night!'

'Now it's your turn, Driftwood' said Glummit cheerily. 'Only we 'ave to get more of a move on with you — because I guess Mr Fowler Sir, you'll find it more amusin' if Driftwood gets turned to quartz first. That'll give Princess Sorrel somethin' to watch in case she gets bored waitin' for the drops to fall.'

'Now, young Driftwood, you come over 'ere an' stan' up against this stalagmite. Didn't know I was educated did you? I know a bit about potholes an' stalactites an' things.'

'I can walk for myself' said Driftwood with a show of nonchalance. He strolled towards the stalagmite which was very near the crater of the pool of Dreadwater. As he did so he made a great yawn, as though bored with the whole performance. He politely put his hand in front of his mouth and then took his place meekly enough where Glummit was pointing.

From now on Driftwood could not speak. He was silent because when he yawned he had transferred the pearl he had been clutching in his fist into his mouth. He knew with certainty that he had a duty beyond any other. He couldn't understand what was going on.

Chuckle and Calm had not arrived to rescue him. The Daylord didn't seem to be able to do anything to answer his cries for help. Sorrel was doomed. Strug and Stumble were imprisoned somewhere in the state rooms above his head. He would soon be bound hand and foot. Yet he still had the pearl and while he had it, there was still hope.

'Hold fast till ...' That was his duty. But till what? If he held the pearl in his hands, they would be bound to see it when they tied him up. It would be wrenched from him. Perhaps if he held it in his mouth he could hold it undetected. Then if he were turned into quartz the pearl would still be safe. There was no question of swallowing the pearl, it was now too large, but it fitted his mouth like a large marble. It was the best he could do.

Fowler seemed to have a special hatred for Driftwood. He came forward and took over from Glummit.

'Tie him up!' he snarled. Dreirds pushed him towards the stalagmite and strapped him against it. He was helpless.

'Look up, Driftwood' commanded Fowler. Immediately above his head was a stalactite.

'Watch carefully' said Fowler. 'You will see the drip beginning to form.'

Indeed the tip of the stalactite was already moist. The drop was small as yet, but it would increase steadily till it fell on him — only one tiny drip, but it would be the end.

'One drop falls every ten minutes' Fowler told him 'You have less than five minutes to go.'

'Be brave Driftwood' called Sorrel from her prison. She was clinging to the bars. 'Remember the Daylord.'

Driftwood would not give Fowler the pleasure of showing fear and forced himself to stand erect and still. He called on the Daylord in his mind and remembered one of the songs at Dove Cottage. He began to let the tune run through his mind.

Suddenly the words, 'Four carpenters to fray' came to him. He remembered Sorrel warbling the tune she had learned at school. He knew two of the carpenters. But where were they now? Somehow he still believed they would rescue him. Maybe he would have to turn to quartz first, but even if he did, they might be able to save the situation in the end.

Similar thoughts were in Sorrel's mind. Indeed she was not as frightened as Glummit had hoped she would be. She thought of Calm and Spindrift. She thought of the ship people. She thought of the reflection of herself that she had seen in the shield. She thought about the Daylord and went on calling to him in her heart. She thought how fine and courageous Driftwood looked, standing among his enemies. To her surprise she realised that she was feeling happy, almost excited. Suddenly deep inside her she knew that something wonderful was going to happen.

CHAPTER 25
THE FOUNTAIN

'Any second now' said Fowler pleasantly.

It was cruel, for despite himself Driftwood glanced quickly above his head. Sure enough, the great drop was trembling and about to fall. Suddenly a cold splash struck him on the nape of the neck. He lifted his head in astonishment, twisting his head from side to side. The Dreadwater had done him no more harm than a tiny splash of rain! Fowler was furious.

'Cut him loose' he ordered and paced the floor in rage.

'You've found the antidote haven't you? The secret I've been searching for all these years. You've found it, you little wretch. I'll search you from head to toe, I'll shake the secret out of you. If I can't use Dreadwater, there are plenty of other ways to finish you off. Why won't you speak. Tell me what you have done. Tell me the secret.'

Fowler had lost all control of himself. He had Driftwood by the shoulders and was shaking him

violently. Glummit stood back and stroked his moustache. Then he put his head on one side.

'I can tell you where 'es 'iding it, whatever it is' he said. ''es got it in 'is mouth. That's where it is. You just leave it to me sir.'

From an inner pocket Glummit took out a small bottle. Uncorking it, he held it right under Driftwood's nostrils. For one awful moment Driftwood struggled, but the fumes were potent. They were worse than ammonia and as they struck the delicate membranes inside his nose, a tremendous sneeze welled up inside him. He sneezed. The pearl shot from his mouth and hit Glummit in the face.

'Ouch!' said Glummit who dropped the bottle.

Everyone dived for the pearl which was rolling downhill towards the crater. Like a rugby player, Driftwood flung himself on it, but found that he was over the edge and slithering and sliding down towards the sullen waters of Dreadwater. Still clutching the pearl with a grip that would never let go, he hit the surface with a splash and went under. The brilliance around him made him open his eyes. Bubbles were streaming up all around him. The water was clear and fresh and as he hit the surface, it looked like a crystal lake.

'The pearl heals the waters.' The truth dawned on him. 'That was why I was sent to Diamede — to heal the waters.'

The pearl was growing at a phenomenal rate. It seemed to feed on the water, for it was already too big to contain in one hand and was still growing. Desperately he tried to hold onto it, but within seconds it was too large for him to get his arms round and so smooth that it was bound to slip through his grasp. As he released the pearl, it plunged down into the blue depths. The water was effervescing now. Huge bubbles were foaming upwards and breaking on the surface in sparkling bursts of mist. Driftwood felt the upward rush all around him. It was a delightful sensation, but he was already struggling to climb up from the crater.

'Here, catch this!' called a friendly voice.

Looking up, Driftwood saw the face of a Dreird. The dullness had gone from the man's eyes and he was dangling a rope by which Driftwood could climb the side of the crater. The whole cavern was full of spray and mist from the foaming, bubbling waters. As the mist drenched down, every Dreird was returning to normal consciousness. The effect of the Dreadwater was being rapidly neutralised. Stalactites and stalagmites were melting like icicles when the thaw begins. Former Dreirds, now neighbourly and kind men, were hurriedly releasing Sorrel from her prison chamber and setting her free.

'Quickly,' shouted a commanding voice. 'Run for it everyone! Don't look back! Don't try to take anything with you! There's not a moment to lose.'

The appearance of the water in the crater was like a boiling cauldron, except that instead of heat there was light. It was beautiful and awe inspiring and in the centre of the pool the ferment was increasing. Suddenly, with an explosive roar, a fountain jet of water leaped towards the ceiling of the cavern. Torrents of water ran everywhere.

Glummit, who had already escaped from the cave lingered in the upper halls of the palace. He knew that Fowler had collected untold heaps of treasure in those rooms and he ran from drawer to drawer, stuffing his pockets full of jewellery and gold.

'Terrible waste!' he groaned to himself. 'Glummit my ol' pal, you'll 'av to leave the rest. Get out while the going's good.'

Turning, he ran towards the stairway which led down onto the rope walkway by which Driftwood had been brought to the castle. He had left it too late. With a roar like a mighty earthquake, the walls of the castle split apart and the sparkling water swept over the sides of the rock like a great waterfall. The flood overtook Glummit and carried him away into the deep ocean. Glummit couldn't swim and the weight of gold and jewels in his pockets carried his corpse down into the depths where it was never seen again.

Driftwood had reached one of the passageways out of the cavern when he felt someone's hand clutch hold of his ankle in a vice like grip.

'If I die, you die with me' Fowler hissed. 'There shall be no escape for either of us.'

'I don't hate you, Fowler!' cried Driftwood. 'Let me help you. Maybe we can get out together.'

Fowler spat at him, his eyes black with venomous hatred.

'No!' he cried 'I want revenge on you.'

Frantically Driftwood struggled with him and suddenly Fowler screamed with horror.

'The barrier cream!' he shrieked. 'The barrier cream!'

As the spray of the pearl fountain washed over him he began to melt before Driftwood's eyes. First his hands became limp and long like pale sticks of decaying celery. His cruel face became even more distorted — like wax melting in a guttering candle. Then he simply washed away like a yellow stain into the water. Only his cloak, shoes and clothing floated for a while on the surface until they were washed away. Of Fowler no trace remained. Driftwood stood a moment or two staring in horror as the stain soaked across the running floor of the cavern, and was diluted by the rush of foam and spray. There was no hatred in his heart, but nor could he find much pity for someone who had so completely given himself to evil that nothing likeable remained.

Sorrel was staring at the quartz statue of Slobbit as the shower of pearl water soaked down on it. What she expected to see she could not have said. What happened amazed her. As the ungainly monster was drenched in the spray of the fountain, he dropped to all fours and shook himself vigorously. For a moment Sorrel was forced to look away. When she looked again, a large and amiable mastiff was sitting on its haunches in front of her.

'Slobbit?' she said tentatively. The animal was shaking itself violently, ears flapping and water jetting everywhere.

'It is Slobbit' she thought to herself. 'I'm sure it is, but I think he wants to reform.'

She looked at the dog sternly.

'Now you won't be cruel ever again, promise?' The dog lowered its head between its paws and lay down on the floor looking at her with doleful and appealing eyes.

'Very well then. If you are a good faithful dog we'll be friends and I'll give you apple pie.'

The dog wagged its tail with frantic joy and bounded up to follow her from the castle. Sorrel realised that Fowler had lied when he had told Driftwood that his dog had been turned to quartz. The Dreadwater had a strange effect on animals. Fowler's mastiff had been turned into Slobbit and some of the palace cats had become gigantic, cruel, and intelligent. However Fowler had concentrated most on the Dreirds because they were most useful for his purposes.

Now, as the healing water deluged down, most people and most things were returning to normal and other evil things were simply being washed away. There was no panic, but people were running everywhere to escape. It took some time to evacuate the Castle completely. Chuckle and Calm had some of the ship people with them, and Strong and Storm were there as well. The Carpenters rode on horseback, marshalling the crowds and taking care that the last stragglers were helped to escape from the Palace.

Eventually a great jet of sparkling water surged through the roof of Diamede, sweeping the entire castle away. As the jet shot skywards, it fell in silver rain, drenching the towns and villages with sparkling water. The fountain shot still higher, blotting out the sky with a brilliant canopy of water high in the heavens and sending rain and mist further and further out to sea.

Down in Heartsease the houses melted as the healing water touched them, and many things were washed away in the downpours. Precious treasures were swept off in floods, but victims of the Dreadwater were healed and growing things flourished with new life. Not everyone was restored. It depended on their hearts. Those who had deliberately chosen to be wicked remained wicked still. The cruel and the hard hearted perished, but the others survived.

The fountain leaped still higher and the islands were no longer illuminated by the sun, but by the light of the fountain itself. This light was kindly and gentle, like golden spring mornings and autumnal mists. This was the pearl light, the light of the Daylord.

CHAPTER 26
NEW DIAMEDE

*T*he four carpenters were recognised by everyone as being the heralds of the Daylord who were in complete authority. They rode on richly caparisoned horses, each in full regal splendour and they had everything under control. They were still recognisable, but were no longer in disguise. Strong and Storm who had been known as Strug and Stumble, were totally free from the effects of Black Tor and the Dreadwater.

One of the heralds' first duties was to rescue the King and Queen. Sorrel was there to welcome her parents as they returned to life. And Slobbit was beside her, wagging his tail with delight and panting happily. Naturally it came as a great surprise to the royal couple to discover that they had been the victims of treachery and that the baby they had known and loved had grown into a beautiful young princess.

Truth to say, Queen Threld remained a little sad about having missed the early years of Sorrel's life, whereas the King seemed well able to cope with the disappointment.

'Consider this, my dear' he pointed out. 'You haven't grown any older while you have been turned to quartz. If Fowler had gone on a few more years, Sorrel might have been older than her mother!'

Amidst all the celebration and excitement, the royal family were soon embracing one another and laughing and crying together as they tried to adjust to the changed situation.

'Just think of it, my darling' said King Threld, 'that wicked villain had the audacity to put you in a crate and carry you about like a bit of furniture. What a mercy you weren't damaged in transit!'

'Would you still love me if I'd been chipped?' the Queen asked roguishly.

'I would still love you even if you were cracked!' announced her husband magnanimously.

Sorrel giggled and Slobbit chose that moment to have a good scratch.

With the wise and powerful royal carpenters to oversee things, the transformation of the city was a joy to watch. It was a delight to see Dreirds returning to normal kindly men and women, and hunting cats becoming contented household pets. Even the carpenters themselves were joyful and enthusiastic as they held back the crowds and saw to all the details of establishing peace and good order in the land.

Out at sea ships were arriving from all directions. They were decked out with bunting, the mariners cheering, saluting, beating drums, sounding fanfares with trumpets and waving their golden shields in the light of the fountain. The blue water of the deep ocean seemed bejewelled with flashing gold like sequins on a rich gown. Dawn and Zoe came to shore with the company from Sorrel's ship.

'We really can be your ladies in waiting now!' exclaimed Zoe.

'I'd rather have you as my sisters' said Sorrel.

Melody and Harmony came with Melody's son who was the Captain of the ship. They'd left Dove Cottage at the Daylord's call.

'When the royal celebrations are over, you and Driftwood must come and have a proper holiday at Dove Cottage' said Melody. 'You left in too much of a hurry last time!'

'There's such a lot I still don't understand' said Sorrel. 'I'm pleased the ships were there, but why did they have to come? How much did you and Harmony know about what was going to happen?'

Melody smiled. 'We didn't know everything and we still don't know all there is to know. That's because what happens to us and these tiny islands is only a part of something much bigger. This is our tale, but it's not the whole story. Every shield and every ship has a story of great adventures, but I can tell you this much about the ships and their shields. They are part of the bigger battle that goes on. Just as there are many islands in our seas, so there are many forces and powers. Some are visible but the strongest are invisible. Dark forces would have helped Fowler, but the light flashing from the shields blinded their eyes. The light flashing from the shields was like a beacon to guide the mighty invisible forces of light as they swept over our islands.

The four carpenters belong to those forces and they have responsibility for our islands, but there are many more besides them. I asked Calm one day how many there were. He said that in his regiment alone there were more than all the stars in our sky.'

'But if there are such great forces I don't see why the Daylord needs ships and shields — or even us' Sorrel declared.

'Quite right ' said Melody. 'I don't suppose the Daylord does need any of us, not even the four carpenters. He could have dealt with Fowler without any help at all. But I'm so glad he worked it out this way, aren't you? The way that the Daylord chooses is always the best way in the end.'

'I've never been so happy in my life' said Sorrel. 'And the best part of it isn't the lovely things I'm being given, it's having friends, being loved and enjoying the Daylord's kindness too. I wish the Daylord would come so that we could see him. I want to thank him over and over again for making me so happy.'

'He will come one day — in the end' replied Melody. 'When the ships have sailed through all the oceans; when the light of the shields has shone in all places of darkness; when everything is in place as it should be, then he will be seen on his throne and all wrongs will be righted and everyone will give him honour. Our part of the pattern is finished, but the weaving is still on the loom — fast though the shuttle flies.'

Chuckle had provided Driftwood with brand new clothes to wear. Sorrel hardly recognised the splendid young man in the robes of a royal nobleman who came to be introduced to her. Driftwood was honoured by King Threld for having been the pearl bearer and it was agreed that he should be treated as a royal prince and welcomed as a member of the family.

Everyone understood that the Daylord still belonged to another place and another time. But they were sure that he knew everything that was going on and that he smiled with approval. It was left to the four Carpenters to be his special representatives, and to sound the trumpets to welcome the dawn of New Diamede. King and Queen Threld would continue to rule justly, wisely and well. Driftwood and Sorrel would share in their reign.

The biggest surprise for everyone was what happened to Black Tor. Even the carpenters had expected that New Diamede would arise out of the sea to take the place of old Diamede. They found, to their surprise that the fountain was always leaping higher and higher and becoming increasingly beautiful. There would be no room for a castle in a place of such magnificent power and splendour.

The sound of the upward rushing mighty waters was deafening as the water shot higher and higher. The canopy of the fountain spread over all the lands and enveloped Black Tor in its spray. Then as the Tor itself ran with living waters, the old grey rocks became white as pearl and full of precious stones.

'It's to be the Palace!' cried Strong.

'Aye' agreed Calm "tis beautiful to behold, but we can improve it yet. This is why all we four Carpenters were needed.'

Chuckle turned to King Threld. 'Aye Sire, all shall be accomplished within three days and three nights. For we are royal carpenters and we work with a will. We shall shape you such a Palace that old Diamede will seem ugly by comparison.'

'Will it still be a place of terrors?' asked Queen Threld.

'Not now the healing waters have touched you' said Calm. 'The Tor will never change. Its power comes from the Daylord himself. But that power adds strength to those who love the Daylord.'

'Nor will it ever cause us to forget who we are' said Strong. 'But it may be that in time it will cause you to forget all sorrow and remember only the good things and the great joys.'

For three days and three nights the royal party travelled in state towards New Diamede. A great armada of ships sailed right round the island to guard the seas. During those three days and nights the fountain leaped higher and higher, spreading its healing touch further and further. Men almost forgot that they were living under the canopy of the fountain, but everywhere the glorious light of the Daylord was bringing happiness and truth.

Then came the glorious day when the four carpenters rode forth from the stately magnificence of New Diamede to greet the royal party. Riding on their magnificent horses, they raised golden trumpets to their lips. Each trumpet had a banner attached to it. The colour of the banner was the same colour as that of the aprons the carpenters had worn: crimson, emerald, sapphire and gold. They sounded a wonderful fanfare and all the attending crowds and the ships out to sea raised a great shout of joy and welcome.

The great Palace of New Diamede stood on the dazzling pearl mountain which had once been Black Tor. The banqueting hall was full of laughter and joy. Chandeliers sparkled and blazed. Beautiful gowns swished across the floor. Men wore splendid uniforms, and the ladies, exquisite dresses. Out on the balconies, spectators could stand to view the great leaping column of the fountain of the pearl. It showed every colour of the rainbow and other shades never seen before. It sparkled and shone, awesome and magnificent. Its sound was like distant thunders, mingled with the richest notes of music. And when men tried to look above it to the arch of its canopy over them, all they could see were rainbows and a brilliance of glory more splendid than the fairest dawn. Even as the feasting and celebration continued, the fountain leaped higher and higher till far off lands received its healing too.

Driftwood and Sorrel had their heads together and were whispering at the banqueting table.

'Will it always be as good as this?' asked Driftwood.

Sorrel shook her head. 'Of course not, silly. This is just the beginning. It will always be better and better. The kingdom will go on growing and growing.'

'I keep thinking about the dinghy' said Driftwood. 'I want to go and see that it's all right. Will you be allowed to sail with me now that you're a princess?'

'Of course' said Sorrel. 'There's going to be plenty of opportunity for more adventures — only our adventures will all be good ones. Life isn't going to get boring now. As the fountain goes higher, life will open out more and more. This is just like the first bud that opens up into blossoms. But the flower will never fade. Instead there will be more buds and more blossoms — till everywhere is full of flowers and fragrance. But listen Driftwood. Listen to the music they're playing. Everyone's joining in the dancing. Let's go and enjoy ourselves with them.'